THE GUARDIANS OF EARTH

THE CHRONICLES OF VIYAN & SAMARA

PRINISHA DEVI

This book is dedicated to all the *Lost Souls* …
Your purposed future is about to unfold …
But only when you believe it true.
The answers lie within you.

And for *Tushani*,
without whose unwavering support,
this book would not have made it to print.

Ever felt that you were meant for more ...
A nagging feeling deep at your core?
Yet this feeling could not find feet in this world,
Like from another realm it was hurled.
Gripping, tugging at you from another place,
Another time, another space.
Or perhaps it is within this world which you live,
Except its illusion holds you captive,
So that you cannot see, what is your true reality.

The Earthly realm is filled with wonder,
Miracles and magic overlooked through sunder.
Yet these exist in plain sight,
In the duality of day and night.
The miracles continue to be,
All we have to do, is look, to see.
Let go of the fear that clouds your vision,
And you can view clearly, your purpose, your mission.

You are a Warrior, a Defender, a Guardian true,
Constructed in strength, credence and virtue.
Believe in yourself for you are meant for more.
Beyond the bounds of this reality lies a magic door,
That leads to your wildest dreams.
And though, while impossible it seems,
You are powerful beyond measure, do not give in,
You are built for greatness, you are going to win.
Triumph in this battle, you will succeed.
So long as you have faith - as long as you believe.

Prologue

The Guardians stood side by side on the battleground. Each of their existences purposed for this very moment. Whatever lives they lived before this, whatever their experiences, it was all a piece to a puzzle. A picture that was now clear since all of its parts were finally connected.

Viyan, Samara, Catori, Liam, Nereida, Yayali, Yana and Ramiel, each concealing one of Durga's weapons, were saving the World, and yet the World would never know. This was their destiny and whether anyone else knew of their heroism was insignificant. As long as they won the battle no one would be the wiser. And that was the plan. They were fulfilling a calling - a prophecy that predated their existence and the only thing that mattered was that they triumphed. The vanquishing of *Rahu*, the dark cosmic energy, would result in the saving of the Earth.

The magical wonder of the Earthly realm is what Viyan and Samara were awoken to through their journey to save her. A World which existed in plain sight, yet one which not everyone could see. This journey unravelled their every understanding of life and defied all logic. But it was this necessary unravelling that opened them up to their possibilities and which triggered their belief in their purpose and belief in themselves. Their very own conviction would become their most powerful weapon.

But would it be powerful enough to destroy *The Threat* and all of its negative usurping energy?

Contents

Chapter One

Extraordinarily Ordinary

"Ok Mara, I had to pull a couple of strings to get you a job here. Please don't mess it up! This is your first job, I know, but I need you to take it seriously because my reputation is at stake," Viyan lectured Samara.

He was rather serious and Samara, well, she was not. Like a good big brother, he constantly covered for his mischievous little sister. He had been protecting her since the day she was born and always prioritised her, no matter how mean or cold she was to him.

Viyan had just completed his third year of engineering at university. He had also been promoted to manager at the department store where he had been working for the past four years. His promotion was a big deal and that is why he needed Samara to take her job seriously. It could not look like he was using his rank to get his little sister, still in school, a job for the summer.

Their mom had suggested that Samara find a job during the summer vacation to expose her to work and to career options. After the summer she would enter her final year at school and so the break allowed for time to figure things out. She had no plans to rush off to university like Viyan had.

In fact, she didn't even know if she wanted to study further. Everyone else seemed to have it all figured out. Her school friends had applied to study straight after graduation and they all knew what they wanted to do with their lives. Those that were not planning on studying already had jobs in mind. While she knew what she didn't want to do, it did not help her much because she didn't know what she did want. And although working under her brother's management was not something that she wanted, better a taste of the working world now than later as a last resort.

Samara wished she had more direction in her life, but unlike most, she honestly could not picture her future. She had no plans or dreams for it. The only word that she could find to describe her situation, was *stuck*. Little did she know how all of that was about to change. That she was soon to become a part of a world that was at the moment oblivious to her. That her reality was to be flipped upside down and that all of the gnawing confusion and insecurity would soon become insignificant. And most importantly, that she would no longer feel misplaced in the world. Her purposed future, the one that felt unpromised, was about to unfold.

"Ok Viyan, I got it, I won't let you down!" Samara assured him as she took her name badge. The two were close and even though they occasionally fought, were more like best friends since they were little. They had a functional dynamic - Samara always got into trouble and Viyan was always there to bail her out. And as independent as she was, it was different when it came to Viyan, she always let him protect her.

"Glad to see that you made it to your first day of work pipsqueak," Viyan's friend, Zayne, smirked as he tousled her loose hair. Samara batted him off. Zayne, Kevin and Viyan had been friends since their first day at school. The siblings were born in Johannesburg, South Africa, but when Viyan was seven and Samara was three, their family relocated to Florida in the United States because of their dad's job transfer. Viyan was sociable and always made friends easily. The three boys took to each other instantly and remained the best of friends through the years. Samara, on the other hand, did not make friends that easily. She did have friends, but not the kind that Viyan had. Her friends, no matter how close they would be, never seemed to stay apart of her life as his had.

That morning Zayne had made his own way to work and was excited to help Samara settle in when he arrived.

"Ok Sam, let me show you around." He led Samara to the aisles to demonstrate what she needed to do. "You just have to ensure that the merchandise is always stocked correctly. You will be assigned to this area," Zayne pointed, indicating the home décor section.

"This is going to be a long week!" Samara sighed.

"Look Sam, this is just the start, if you can show that you're dedicated and help the customers, then you can move to another section within a few weeks. Just prove to be a good worker, it's not rocket science."

"And therein lies the problem," she retorted.

Zayne raised his eyebrows as he left to do his work.

"This place is not that bad, and who knows, you may even make some friends," he shouted as he walked away.

Samara wasn't looking to make new friends, they kind of didn't stick around that long anyway. For her, 'best' friends came and went, so she got used to the idea that while she would have friends, her friendships could not be the type that she longed for. She just had to keep reminding herself not to get too emotionally close because if she did, she would only end up getting hurt.

The end of the day came quicker than expected.

"So how was your first day Sam?" Zayne asked as he jumped into the car.

"Honestly, it wasn't as bad as I thought. I am tired though."

"You get used to it. It's a shock to the system at first when you enter the working world. Becoming responsible and adult-like can be confusing but, it literally grows on you … or you grow into it."

Zayne paused as he stared glumly out the window. He then continued, getting slower and more sombre with each sentence.

"You kinda don't have a choice really. You, are officially, no longer, young. Welcome to the rest of your boring life."

"Hey, it's not that bad, he is just messing with you," Viyan cut in. "Besides, when you get that first paycheck, it will all be worth it!" He winked at Samara before stopping the car to turn to the back seat. "And speaking of paycheck, I believe you owe me some money."

"Well, this is me! I'll see you tomorrow," Zayne said, quickly jumping out of the car. They had stopped at his house to drop him off and then they headed home to theirs.

The siblings reached home and went upstairs to their rooms to wash away the tiredness of the workday. It was already 7 p.m. and their mum was in the kitchen making dinner. When the food was ready, she called them down to eat. Their dad hadn't gotten home from work as yet so the three of them sat down for dinner as they did every evening.

"Finally! I am starving!" Samara exclaimed as she pulled her chair closer toward the table.

"And? How was the first day?" Mum asked.

Samara was quiet, she was too busy gobbling down her food.

"My gosh, you would think that you had travelled to space and haven't seen food for months. It's just the first day!" Viyan laughed as Samara stuffed her mouth.

"Yes, work will do that to you," their mum sighed.

"I once used to look like you," she raised her eyebrows at Samara.

"And then I started to work, and now I look like this."

They all laughed.

"Well then I have nothing to worry about," Samara said with a smile to her before asking, "Please pass the potatoes."

As she added potatoes to her plate, she told her mother about her first day. "Work was not as bad as I thought, but let's check-in at the end of the week."

The next morning, Samara reluctantly got ready for work and went downstairs for breakfast. She sat at the kitchen table and yawned widely.

"Don't worry, you'll get used to getting up early… eventually," Viyan said with a side smile. "Grab something to eat, we leave in ten."

She poured cereal into a bowl.

"Here you go!" Viyan handed her a packed lunch.

"Let's hope this can take you through the day. We can't let **Mom** think that you're slave driven at work. Not after last night."

Zayne lived three streets away and they picked him up before heading to work. "You made it to your second day! Well done! I wasn't sure if I would be seeing you today," Zayne grinned as he jumped into the car.

"I wasn't sure if I'd make it either! But let's see how today goes, tomorrow could be that day. These working hours are really clashing with my beauty sleep."

She joked, but Samara really was beautiful, she just never thought of herself as such. Her *simply ordinary* self-description was flawed. Small, almond-shaped eyes were flattered with striking lashes. A button nose and pinkish-brown, bow-shaped lips along with a pronounced chin, featured within a heart-shaped face. Her brown complexion, with a tinge of yellow undertone, was complimented by her long, wavy, dark hair.

They worked a 9 to 5 shift, but because Viyan was now the manager, they were in half an hour earlier.

"Can I get an extra hour at lunchtime to nap for coming in early?" Samara asked, yawning as they jumped out of the car.

"Good luck with that," Zayne sneered. "I have been asking ever since he got promoted. There really aren't any perks to being friends with the manager," he said, shaking his head as he walked off to his department.

The first week was good. Samara was getting accustomed to everything and to the people. She settled in quickly, but it was not too stimulating and became mundane by the following week. Viyan was the one that was book smart, he worked hard and got good grades, and he always took a liking to school. While Samara did not always get the highest marks, she was highly intelligent, just easily bored. Her mind would wander.

She had an active imagination and as her mom would often say, *she always had her head up in the clouds*. This however, was never a bad thing in their home because she was a problem solver.

One day at work, when her tasks were complete and she did not have anything to do, she began to contemplate her life. What was she going to do with hers? As she walked through the aisles, she questioned herself, trying to piece everything together.

"I just don't know. For the longest time I have never dreamed about a particular career. I also know that I can't do this for the rest of my life. It's just not for me. What am I supposed to do?" she asked out aloud, talking to herself as she often did.

She heard a whisper coming from behind her.

"You'll know soon enough".

Startled, she turned around, but there was no one there.

"*Hi?*" she called out while surveying the surroundings.

There was no one around her. In fact, it was oddly quiet.

"Ok, I am laying off the self-talk, it's now moving on to a full-blown conversation!" she exclaimed as she shook her head.

The day usually hit a slump when they had very few customers. An afternoon after her lunch break Samara lay on one of the display beds to rest, but she fell asleep instead and began to dream. She saw a beautiful lady with long locks of hair, draped in a red and yellow sari and adorned with shiny gold jewellery. The lady was tall, twice her height, and Samara felt like a little girl in her presence. It was a dream, but it felt so real. The lady slowly approached her and bent down to whisper in her ear, but Samara could not make out what was being said. She tried to listen closely and just as the whispers became audible, the woman pulled away and smiled at her. As Samara looked into her eyes, she jolted awake.

Samara was completely disorientated once she came to and had to gain her bearings. It didn't feel like a dream at all, in fact, she was not sure if it had just happened. She tried to recollect her dream. Samara felt as though she knew the lady, she seemed strangely familiar. She resembled a *Hindu goddess*, but she felt human, as if Samara physically felt her presence in the dream. It was all so real, yet it was not. Her dreams were never vivid, she usually never even remembered them. But this one…it haunted her.

The rest of the week passed with no strange dreams or anything out of the ordinary. Her life resumed its normal course and by the end of the week, she had even forgotten about the dream and was back to her sarcastic self. Samara began to make friends at work that she would hang out with during her breaks. She hated to admit it but Zayne called it, she did enjoy their company. She even found a connection with one of the girls. Megan was a year older and had decided to skip studying after high school. The two of them clicked; they had a lot in common and thought alike. They began to spend all their free time at work together.

"Oh, my gosh!" exclaimed Megan as she joined Samara for lunch at the canteen. She laid down her tray and sat on the chair across from Samara, "I had to deal with such an annoying customer earlier."

"Really? Ok, lemme guess! It was an older man. He was looking for a gift for his wife. He kept on asking you to explain how almost all of the products work, in detail. And then he bought … nothing."

"That was exactly what happened!" Megan declared as she rolled her eyes. "I was like, thank you sir but I have other customers to attend to."

"You said that?!"

"Of course not, because I didn't. Please swap departments with me," Megan begged.

"What's in it for me?"

"All the sweet, kind, caring, old, rich men that need assistance with shopping."

"That's a hard pass!" Samara said shaking her head.

"Think of the commission," Megan tempted her.

Samara thought for a second, "Nah, not worth it."

"Well, worth a try," Megan said before they both laughed.

The two spent a lot of the day analysing the odd behaviour of the customers, pretending to be Psychology majors collecting data for their theses. Samara had made a close friend in the short space of time; Megan confided everything in her and they were inseparable at work. They would even text each other after work and laugh about the day and the crazy happenings.

The next Monday, Megan broke down when she found Samara at her workstation.

"Charlie is leaving," she sniffed. "He told me that he is going to London on a working programme."

Charlie was Megan's boyfriend.

"Oh no! That is terrible!" exclaimed Samara. She leaned in to hug her, "I am sorry. When did you find out?"

"He came over to my house last night to tell me. He was so casual about it too."

"Well look, it is a shock, I mean you just found out, but it's a good thing. He will get some work experience and it will be better for his employment in the long run." Samara tried to make Megan feel better. "Also, you guys have been dating since like 12. That's a long time! This is a good opportunity to take a break and you guys can pick up when he returns," she advised, wanting to add some positivity to the situation.

"It's not that! He has obviously been considering this for a while. He has done all the applications without even talking to me about it. He knew what he wanted to do and what was happening all this time without even hinting at anything. It's over! He planned to start this new life and not include me in it."

Samara was diplomatic in her response. "I get that you're hurting now but maybe he does have an explanation. I'm giving him the benefit of the doubt but either way, let's not wait around for him to explain. I am taking you out this weekend!" Samara felt so grown up. This was something that her mom would do. She listened to Megan and did not take any sides.

Perhaps I'd make a good therapist, she thought to herself, considering the career path.

Megan slowly stopped crying and began to smile. "You are right! We are still young, and I am not going to cry over someone who didn't have the decency to consider how this would affect me."

"That's the attitude!" Samara nudged her. "But I still think we should go out. You don't deserve to get treated like this."

Megan moved over to hug Samara, "You are such an awesome person, I am lucky to have you. You're like my best friend."

And with those words, Samara melted inside. *Did Megan just call her her best friend?*

Megan was a stylish and attractive girl. The opposite of Megan, Samara did not wear make-up often and was not a *girly-girl*. She did not like to draw attention to herself and preferred to blend in. Secretly though, she wanted to be one of the popular girls, the ones who always dressed so well and had all the boys swoon after them. Someone just like Megan. Because she did not think that she could be that, Samara settled for the stereotypical, girl-next-door persona instead. And, when Megan called her best friend, she felt seen.

Samara distracted Megan from thinking about Charlie by joking around. At first she came across as shy and perhaps even a bit rude, but once you got to know her and she was comfortable around you, Samara was exceptionally entertaining.

"Ok, so what do you want to do this weekend?" she asked Megan. "Want to go to the movies and grab something to eat? Or, you can even just come hang at my house?"

"That sounds fab, we can just chill at the pool with some cocktails and snacks and unwind," Megan said enthusiastically. "Speaking of unwinding, will Viyan be joining us? Now that I'm on the rebound..."

"Ewe! That's so gross!" Samara cut her off. "Don't bring my brother into your post-break-up shenanigans."

"I'm not making any promises. I know you don't see it, but he is a hottie."

Viyan was tall and well built, lean with just enough muscle. He had dark black hair forming from two crowns - one in the centre of his head and one right in the middle of his forehead, where his hairline began; the reason he always naturally had a bedhead look. Dark brown eyes were emphasized by long lashes and full, dark brows. These deep features were softened by a charming smile. Samara just shook her head. The girls did find Viyan handsome, but he was more focused on excelling at work and building his career. The two of them could not be more different. He was studious and focused and she was confused and had a wandering spirit.

It was Friday and the end of the work week. Samara could not wait to just chill and hang out with Megan the next day. But when they got home Megan texted her to say that she couldn't make it, something had come up and she would see her on Monday at work. Samara headed into the kitchen after changing from her work clothes.

"How was your day honey?" her mum asked.

"It was ok. I'm just glad it's the weekend."

"I can't wait to meet Megan tomorrow! I got you guys some snacks."

Her mother pointed to a packet on the kitchen counter, filled with junk food.

"Thanks Mom," Samara said with a grateful smile. "But Megan can't make it tomorrow."

"Great!" Zayne cut in. "I'll just take these then," he said as he looked into the packet of snacks.

"Why are you always here? Eating my food!" Samara sneered at him.

He walked towards Samara's mum. "Because my mom does not love me as much as yours does," he said giving her mother a kiss. Her mum giggled and responded with a hug and a kiss on his cheek.

"Ahhh, that's disappointing. Do you want to do something with me tomorrow instead?"

"Sure, can we go for brunch?"

"It's a date!" her mum winked at her.

She helped her mum and dad prepare dinner while Viyan, Zayne and Kevin watched TV. Once the dinner was ready, they sat at the table to eat together. This was their normal weekend routine; just a regular Friday night before the boys headed out. Samara helped clean up before going to her room. She put on the series that she was catching up on and fell asleep through the first episode.

The next morning, she felt better when she woke, looking forward to the quality time with her mum. They enjoyed a relaxing brunch at a popular coffee shop in the area.

"So Moo, have you considered what you want to do next year?"

Moo was the pet name that they had given Samara when she was a baby. It was based on a television show, *Mina Moo*, that her mum used to watch as a kid. She called her *Mara Moo* and then eventually it became just *Moo*.

"We are already three months into the year. I don't want to pressure you but if you want to attend university, then you need to start applying soon."

"I get it Mom, I need to focus on it, but I still do not know what I want to do with the rest of my life. It's a massive decision and I am not ready to make this life-altering choice," Samara said in a panic.

"Look, I realise that it can be overwhelming, but you need to understand that nothing is fixed, you can always change paths. Do not worry yourself with needing to get into something you will be doing for the rest of your life. Just try to gauge what feels right for you and where you see yourself."

"I know, and thanks for not pushing me on this." She paused and then spoke in a softer, slower tone. "You may think that I don't care about my future, but the truth is that I really do and that's why I don't want to mess it up. I just cannot see myself in anything. I can't seem to feel a connection to what I would like to get into. I HATE not being able to make a decision and just not knowing. While everyone else has it all figured out, I have no idea what I want to do with my life. I feel so … stuck!" Looking down, Samara exhaled a deep breath, feeling hopeless, as if she was the only one who had ever felt this way. "*I feel lost!*"

Sensing that it was making her anxious, her mother eased off.

"Ok, take a little more time but do some research on what options are out there and what you may feel drawn to. Maybe do some volunteer work, that way you can look at different career options."

She paused. "Hey! Why don't you try to get involved in taekwondo again? Maybe you can help with training younger kids? It will help relax your mind with all of this confusion."

Samara had a black belt in taekwondo and her sensei had said that she was naturally gifted in the art. He had even asked her, on more than one occasion, to help him teach.

"Ok Mom, I'll look into it."

Her mother placed her hand on hers and gave her a warm smile.

"I love you," she said.

"I love you more," Samara automatically replied.

"I love you most," her mum ended softly.

They spent the rest of the day together, shopping and enjoying afternoon tea and cake before heading home. Distracted from her worries, it was just what Samara needed.

They took a pizza home for dinner. After helping her mum unpack the car, she headed to the pyjama lounge upstairs to watch a movie. The boys took up their pizza to join her. They put the *X-Men* on. Samara hated watching movies with them because they always debated story plots and character timelines. The boys were seriously into comics but didn't consider themselves comic geeks. Because they were on the school football team in high school, they still tried to maintain their macho images. But this time, their debating would not be the reason that Samara left the room. While watching the movie she was randomly scrolling through her phone when she saw that Megan was tagged in a post. One of Megan's friends had uploaded some photos of them hanging out together. Samara instantly felt a lump in her chest. She stood up to leave.

"Hey, you can have the remote back, don't leave," Zayne offered.

"It's not that, I'm actually super tired. I am going to head to my room," she **said, trying** not to show her change in mood.

"But it's only 8 p.m.! Don't you want to come out with us?" Kevin asked.

"Thanks guys but I am gonna hit the hay. I'll see you tomorrow morning when you get home."

Why couldn't Megan just tell her that she was going out? Samara was the one who suggested that they do something in the first place. *Why didn't Megan invite her?* Samara texted Megan, 'Hope you had a good day' but she didn't get a reply and not one for the rest of the weekend.

When Monday came around Samara tried to avoid Megan at work until she snuck up on her at her station.

"*Hey Sam!*" Megan shouted behind her.

"Oh hey!" Samara pretended to be busy.

"Where have you been the whole morning?"

"Oh, I had to do some stock-taking for Viyan."

Samara lied, trying not to make it obvious that she was avoiding her. She continued to realign the merchandise on the shelf that she had already packed, just so that she did not have to make eye-contact.

"Look I am sorry about this weekend."

"Erh, that's ok!" Samara replied, not wanting to show how much it had bothered her.

"Yeah, I um, I had to help my mom with something."

Samara stopped what she was doing, taken aback by what Megan had just said.

"Oh!?" She didn't know whether to ask more to see why Megan was lying or to just let it go.

"Yeah, sure." She actually didn't want to know. "We can always do it again."

"Ok great!" Megan said, feeling relief from her guilty conscience.

"I promise to warn my mom in advance," she laughed.

Samara said it for the sake of being nonchalant, but she didn't mean it. There was no way that she was opening up to Megan. Never again!

She got that Megan had other friends that she hung out with, she had friends before she met Samara, but why did she have to lie to her? Why did she hide that she was hanging out with her other friends? That hurt, and it made Samara feel like she was not good enough. *Why did this always happen to her?* She always got hurt like this when it came to friends, she would do anything for them, but they never felt the same. *WHY?!*

This played on her mind for the next few days. It was not so much about Megan but about Samara herself. Why could she not keep a friend? Look at Viyan, he had kept the same friends from the very first day that they met, and they were still inseparable. She longed for that kind of friendship, but it never happened to her. Friendships were temporary for her; her friends never stuck around, no matter how close they got. *What was wrong with her?*

There were valid answers to these plaguing questions and they were more profound than she realised.

Samara had an athletic physique, physically strong from all her gymnastics and martial arts training. If you looked at her you would think that she was a popular girl just based on her looks, someone who had a best friend by her side her whole life. Perhaps it was because she always felt this constant rejection, that she never thought she could be anything more than who she was. This self-doubt was the reason for her limbo in life. She was too afraid of rejection and making the wrong choices that she built a wall around herself. But, because of her trusting, innocent nature, this wall kept on crumbling, until she had to rebuild it each time that she got hurt. Again and again, so many times over, that she was no longer sure of who the person inside was that she wanted to protect.

Chapter Two

The Awakening

That night Samara went to bed with a heavy heart. She dreamt, almost instantly, as if someone had felt her pain and was waiting to answer her questions. The beautiful lady came to her once again, but this time she was accompanied by a lion. They both walked slowly toward her, faded at first by mist but becoming clearer as they drew closer. Samara could not physically see herself in the dream, but it was as though she was watching them. She felt her heart begin to beat faster as the lion became more visible. Suddenly the beast was standing beside her, and she froze. Sensing his warm breath on her arm, she felt a shiver run down her spine and she immediately awoke in a panic.

Samara's breathing was fast and heavy – it did not feel like a dream at all. It felt very, very real, and the breath of the lion upon her skin had made the hair on her arms rise. She sat up in bed, in complete disbelief. *Was she going crazy?* This was the second time that she had dreamt of the lady, and not just any lady. Samara knew who She was - She was a Hindu goddess. Although she was not religious, Samara was aware of Hindu gods and goddesses because of her Hindu heritage. She pulled out her tablet and began to research. She surveyed a few images of goddesses and eventually made a match. It was

Goddess Durga. While the Goddess was much more beautiful in her dream, the images Samara found of Her were similar. Similar, except that She did not have as many arms as She did in the depictions of Her. The Goddess was tall, slightly dusky in complexion and She had luscious, rich, black, long locks of hair. She was draped in a beautiful red and yellow sari and also did not have as much jewellery as usually displayed in imagery. She simply wore gold bangles on each arm and a necklace around Her neck. She radiated a golden light that glowed from Her skin.

Samara knew that She was Durga because of the massive lion that accompanied Her. In Hindu mythology, the Goddess Durga was mostly represented with a lion or tiger by Her side. Samara wondered why the Goddess was appearing in her dreams. She tried to read up as much as she could to find the motive for seeing Durga so often, and so vividly. She gathered information feverishly, like a student about to miss an assignment deadline. Eventually she fell asleep and awoke the next morning to Viyan shouting for her to get up for work.

At work, her mind kept drifting back to her dream. She spent her lunch hours that week reading up on Hindu mythology and dreams. Before she knew it, she was way down the rabbit hole, and it introduced her to an entirely different world.

It seemed that Samara was not the only one who had had the same experience. It was as though a *secret society* had existed all this time and she somehow just stumbled upon it now. Though they were not such a secret. There was a plethora of information online as well as numerous social groups dedicated to sharing information. Her world was flipped over. She discovered so much credible evidence to complement the existence of this alternate reality. She became consumed with studying as much as she could. The dreams could not have come at a better time because they also gave her an excuse to avoid Megan.

Samara was never too good at confrontation. She would rather avoid Megan completely than discuss with her what had happened and how she felt. She had lost so many friends along the way that she did not want to seem weak and vulnerable. That was her problem, she always got too close to people too soon and always went against her own better judgement. She would caution herself but at the same time, she was like an innocent child that would just leap into things, seeing the good in everyone. Samara was also very forgiving and that was another reason that she was avoiding Megan. Thus, she buried herself in learning more instead.

Two weeks passed and she did not have any visions or strange dreams. Her life went back to normal. She cut down on the research and it slowly stopped consuming her time, she had even almost forgotten about the dream. Life resumed.

Friday night, after a long week at work, Samara went to bed early. As she rested her head, she went into a deep slumber. Durga visited her again but on this visit, She spoke to her. Samara saw the back of herself in the vision. She was standing in a vast, empty, white space. The Goddess was in the distance, slowly coming toward her. This time however, Samara was not afraid. Remembering what had happened the last time, she thought to herself, *calm down, relax, it is just a dream*. But she was well aware that this was more than *just a dream*. She calmed herself and waited for the Goddess to approach her, however the lion came to meet Samara first instead. She looked straight into his eyes and felt a shiver, not out of fear but because of an exchange of energy, as though he was greeting her. The lion came to rub up against her side as a sign of affection. The Goddess then walked up to Samara, paused and smiled, and Samara instantly felt a warmth and a sense of ease flowing through her.

They walked without saying a word and slowly the scenery around them started to change. The three sauntered through a lush green field, making their way to the bank of a flowing river. Almost at the edge of the field, Samara could smell the fresh water that flowed in the crystal blue river. On the bank of the river stood a huge tree and a few boulders randomly surrounding it. The Goddess sat on a rock and Samara sat on one beside Her, under the shade of the large tree. Durga plucked what looked like a lotus flower from one of the branches. She peeled away the petals and revealed an apple, which She handed to Samara. It was the biggest, reddest apple she had seen. Samara bit into it and tasted the sweetness as the juice trickled down her throat. For the first time since the visions, the Goddess spoke. Her voice was soft and gentle.

"I am so glad that I finally can talk to you."

Samara stared blankly, having no idea what to say or if she could even say anything in response.

Durga nodded, "Yes, you can talk."

With those words, a million questions ran through Samara's mind.

"Or you can think it and I will answer."

The Goddess had such a calming effect.

"Yes, I am Durga," She said with a warm smile.

"You are dreaming, but this is real. All of the other times I wanted to come to you, but you were not ready to meet me. I have come now because you are prepared to accept what I will tell you."

Durga explained to Samara that she needed her to learn that there was more to the World. Being exposed to the notion that life is so much more than the everyday routine that we live, Samara became open to the Goddess' existence. When Samara began to research about Durga, she discovered a whole new world which opened her understanding of the Universe. If Durga had come any sooner though, Samara would have just dismissed Her. She came at a time when Samara was lost and looking for answers. But the Goddess needed her mind to calm down before she returned. Exposure to all the new information she had learnt was clouding her judgment and her intuition.

"Is there anything that you would like to ask?" the Goddess queried.

Still, Samara did not speak. Running through her mind was the uncertainty of why the Goddess came to her. *Was it to help her heal what was hurting?* The Goddess was patient till Samara eventually asked what had weighed heavy on her heart and mind for many years. She spewed the words like a well-rehearsed speech, "People have told me that I am too sensitive, and I have tried to not feel the way I do, trust me, I hate feeling this way, but I have always wanted to know ... *why I am never able to keep friends?* Why do they never stay in my life? I was so sure that Megan was the friend that I longed for. I have had friends in my life, but I have always wanted a best friend beside me, like a sister. I know that I am that friend, that best friend, but why has no one felt that way about me? I don't think that I am a bad person." She paused to think.

"*Am I?*"

Something which had plagued her for so long but that she had learned to hide beneath a nonchalant attitude, had now resurfaced due to Megan's friendship. Durga looked lovingly at Samara and explained that she would make the perfect friend; she was loyal, loving and genuinely cared for people. "And that is why, there is no doubt that you are the protective one and possess all the qualities of a warrior. But it is because you are just that, that we could not allow you to get too close to other people. It would have deterred you from your path, your purpose and your destiny. It is not that you are a terrible friend, but rather that you are too good a friend, and you would have done too much for others. This would mean straying off a path that you were meant to follow."

Samara was confused. What life path was the Goddess talking about?

"You also get too emotionally involved, too quickly. This is your trusting nature and the way everyone should be - *unguarded*. But everyone is not the same and because they are all not like you, the World can be a dangerous place. Losing friends and people close to you made you stronger. It always forced you to become a little more cautious. However, because of your personality, you are only cautious and not closed off."

All of what Samara was hearing was so specific.

"How did you know that what I had experienced would not change who I am as a person? That it would not make me hard and angry at the world?"

"Because no matter what the world throws at you, it will not change who you are at heart. This is the mark of a true leader."

"*Leader?*" Samara asked.

"You are the Defender; it is your destiny! Everything that has happened, has happened for a reason, and it has led you to this exact moment. You are exactly where and *when* you need to be."

Samara was perplexed. The situation was making her anxious and her mind began to race. She knew that she was dreaming but it felt palpable, like she was asleep but conscious. And everything that was transpiring in her dream was a response to her real-life dilemmas. *Was all of this real?*

Sensing her anguish, Durga delicately explained that her destiny was written long before she was born; both hers and Viyan's. The gods knew that a time would come when Earth would be threatened and so they prophesied that *two saviours* would stop the destruction. Because Samara had researched possible realms and alternate universes, she believed what the Goddess told her. In fact, she began to feel a sense of relief. She always knew deep down that she was meant to be more, she constantly had a nagging feeling that she needed to achieve greater with her life. The older she got, the more persistent this feeling became. The question of *what her life's purpose was* grew stronger and she felt this disquieting deep at her core. It was the very reason that she did not know what to do with her future, why she was at crossroads in choosing a career, and her life in general. She felt comforted that that confusion was finally being validated, that there was a reason for it - a purpose.

Samara asked, "If the gods knew about the threat, why did they not change the course of events? Why do they not stop it themselves? Surely they have the power to do so. Or, why do they not just come to Earth and eliminate the threat?"

"Because neither I nor any god can. It is a very delicate balance that we must maintain. The gods simply watch over the Universe, and Earth is just one inhabited planet in the vast Cosmos. Planets are governed by their own races and the gods cannot intervene. We have however tried to guide man, but not in our capacity as gods. To guide without any influence of power, we *became Man to help Man*. Across time and cultures and religions, we have incarnated on Earth in human form. We have tried to guide humans on the right path to goodness. We did not do it with power or force because Man has the choice of how to live their life on Earth."

Durga paused and smiled at Samara as if the next part was meant for her.

"It is every human's destiny to live their own lives and learn their lessons. This is every soul's fate; every individual must undergo their own journey. They are guided along the way but ultimately, they need to make their own decisions. This is the *human experience* - for every person to live life through an individual experience of the World, and in so doing, learn the lessons that come with it. Hence, we gods cannot intervene because this will defeat the soul's objective. However, the *shared human experience* is a way for humans to help each other in their journeys. Since everyone's life will not be the same, the objective was for humans to share the knowledge gained from their existence on Earth so that they could have a collective experience of life."

She paused again.

"When a threat of this magnitude is to befall a planet, and there seems to be no alternative, the gods cannot allow the destruction of the whole race. That is why you, Samara, were chosen. But you, like any human, still have free will to decide if you do not want to fulfil your destiny, now that you have learnt what it is."

"*Free will?*" Samara asked.

"Well, your life path has been planned, you are the one we have selected lifetime after lifetime to save the World, but you ultimately can decide not to go ahead with the plan."

Durga looked at Samara and smiled. "I must have confused you by saying lifetime after lifetime. You see, you have lived on Earth before, and both you and Viyan have always incarnated together, training for this very event. You in your physical form may not remember, but your soul does. You both have been living for this mission over many lifetimes, learning and experiencing lessons as you journey."

Durga gave Samara time to unpack the information that she had conveyed.

"Centuries ago, a human created from my likeness was born. I could not come to Earth to protect it, so I created someone like me who could. You are that very someone. *A human to defend humanity.* You both have never been alone in this though. When we gods knew about what would happen in the future, we came together to form the ones who would protect the Earth. You, Viyan and a few other chosen ones were given qualities - powers as you would say, for you to take on this task. With each life lived these powers became stronger. You just need to remember your gifts."

Since the dawn of the new Earth, the gods created creatures to protect her. These life forms existed long before present-day humans did. When humans were born into the World, the protectors were then tasked to not only guard the Earth but to guide the humans too. With the foretelling of the eminent threat to the Earth, these creatures, along with Samara and Viyan, were destined to become *The Guardians of Earth*. A representative from each of the intelligent races across time on Earth was selected to protect Her. They fought many battles along the way, but all were ultimately leading up to the present mission. Each creature yields a sacred weapon given to them by the gods and necessary to protect the Earth. They all lay in hiding, awaiting that predestined day and ultimately, Samara and Viyan's unification of them.

"Before I leave you, do you have any more questions?" the Goddess asked. Samara thought of something that had confused her while she was researching. She asked Durga why She was sometimes seen with a tiger and sometimes a lion. In Her portrayals, Durga was often depicted with a tiger, but She came to Samara with a lion as a companion.

"Both beasts are majestic. Just as I come to you in these visions, throughout the history of man I have done the same for many. To guide and give direction I, as with many other god forms, have come in visions. Some remembered a tiger, others a lion, and this is how they shared my image with the rest. For some, the lion seemed to hold more strength whereas the tiger felt calmer for the others, and it was what they connected with. In your case it is a *lion*," Durga replied smiling as She touched the head of the beast beside Her.

The truth was that Samara envisioned the form of the lion because that is what resonated with her. The lion represented her African roots. The siblings were meant to live in Africa, but their parents decided to move away to protect them both. The prophecy foretold that the *Protector would come from Africa* and that is why they were at risk if they remained there. Africa was in Samara's blood and very much who she was. It was the reason that she connected with the lion and partially why she never truly felt *at home* growing up.

"We have spent hours talking, it is time that I left you," Durga said to her.

"How will I know what to do from here? Do I just carry on with life normally? Do I pretend that this did not happen? You said that I am the defender, but I have no idea what I need to do and who I need to defend?"

As Samara threw the questions at the Goddess, Durga leaned toward her and smiled, "Everything will fall into place soon enough." She then whispered, "But only when you truly believe."

Abruptly Samara awoke. She sat back in her bed and absorbed everything that had just happened. She turned to look at her clock, hours must have passed, it should be morning already. Strangely, only an hour had gone by. Samara jumped up and ran to look for Viyan, but it was Friday night and he was out with the boys. She went down to the kitchen to make herself a cup of rooibos tea and tried to get back to bed. It was all too overwhelming to comprehend.

The next morning, she was in the middle of her cereal when Viyan came down to the kitchen. He began to pour himself a cup of coffee and when he turned around, he caught Samara staring at him.

"Good morning?" he said confused.

"Hi!" Samara smiled back.

As he went over to the counter to look at what his mum had cooked, he caught Samara staring at him from the corner of her eye.

"Ok, what's up?" he asked.

"Nothing!"

She paused, then blurted, "Did you … by any chance… have a … weird dream last night? Like about a goddess and a destiny?"

"Huh?" Viyan replied confused.

"Yeah, yeah, never mind."

Samara tried to change the subject, "So what did you guys do last night?"

Monday morning Viyan was late to come down for breakfast. Viyan was never late! Samara was already eating her cereal when he walked into the kitchen.

"Morning!" she said cheerfully.

"Morning," he replied distracted.

Samara continued to eat her breakfast while scrolling through her phone. She could feel Viyan staring at her but when she looked up, he immediately looked away. She continued on her phone and when she looked up again, he was staring at her before diverting his gaze.

"Okay, what's up?" she asked as she put down her phone to look at him.

He went to sit down beside her.

"So … remember when you asked me if I had a strange dream about a goddess?"

"Uh-huh!" Samara shook her head while taking in a mouthful of cereal.

"What if I did?" he asked her slowly.

"I would ask you to elaborate."

"Well, I don't know how to explain it. And actually, I would not have thought too much about it if you did not mention it to me the other day."

He paused before continuing.

"This beautiful Hindu goddess came to me in a dream. She whispered something in my ear, but I could not make out what She was saying. It was strange because I then felt something warm against my arm and when I turned to the side, there was an enormous lion beside me. I woke in a panic because it all felt so real."

Samara just smiled, "Did he come up and smell you?"

"Yes! He did!"

"But that's not the weirdest part," he continued. "I fell asleep again after trying to process it all and I began to instantly dream. This time the Goddess spoke to me." He stopped. "Look, this may all sound really crazy, but it felt like an actual conversation and I remember it all so clearly, not like in a dream where everything is jumbled up. I remember what She said to me and it's insane!" He stopped again.

"It's all right, you can tell me, trust me I will not judge you," Samara assured him.

"Ok! So, basically She said that you and I … are meant to save the Earth."

"No, no," Samara interrupted him. "I want the long version."

Viyan exhaled loudly and began to explain in more detail.

"When I fell asleep the second time, the Goddess guided me on a pathway which led to a large, colourful garden. We walked toward a large apple tree that stood on the bank of a small river. Everything was so bright and lush and I could feel all the colourful energy in my dream. We sat down beneath the tree and She plucked an apple from it and handed it to me. It was so red! I bit into it and could taste the sweet apple juice – it was delicious. As I took a second bite She began to talk." He stopped to think before starting again. "You know I didn't ask her who She was, I just knew that She was a Hindu goddess."

"She's Durga. I asked," Samara said, nodding her head proudly.

"Of course you did!" Viyan snickered.

"The Goddess began to speak to me and everything She said thereafter was like a fantasy. She said that we were sitting under the *Tree of Knowledge* and that I was just like the tree. My name, *Viyan,* means *special knowledge* and I was gifted with this, but there is so much that I am yet to uncover. She explained that you and I had lived many lifetimes before, acquiring the knowledge and skills to use in this lifetime. We are …" he stopped for a bit. "You know, I don't know what to make of this, but apparently you and I are meant to save the Earth. I don't understand what that means."

He leaned closer to Samara. "Look Mara, I would have just brushed this off but it felt so real, it did not feel like a dream at all. And then, you mentioned that you dreamt about a goddess too. I mean, is this a coincidence? Did I create all of this in my mind because you mentioned it? I am so confused!"

"You could have, but how do you explain that we had the exact same dream without you knowing the in-depth details of mine?" she said to ease his mind.

During the workday, Viyan kept on popping up at her station to ask about something that he had thought of. He was like a kid that had just watched a movie and was putting all the pieces together as the day progressed.

Later in the day Viyan met Zayne for lunch. They sat outside on the rooftop where it was quiet. They often did this to escape the busyness of the store and to clear their heads. As they both sat on the ledge, looking off into the distance, Viyan turned to Zayne to ask, "Ever think that there was more to life? Like, everything that we are living is an illusion. None of this - school, work and our daily existence - is what life is really about."

He paused. "It is all a mask to what our purpose as humans actually is. None of this is real."

Zayne looked at him with a blank face, "A tad bit philosophical for a Monday bud! I think Sam is finally rubbing off on you," he joked.

Viyan laughed, "You're right," he said, nodding his head.

He opened his lunch, embarrassed for being so vulnerable.

There was silence as they began to eat.

"Honestly though," Zayne said, breaking the silence. "I have thought about life's purpose before and wondered if there was more to all this," he expressed, gesturing with his hands to the view. "But then how would you explain life expansion, technology or global growth and development? Why would our world be this which we are living in. Why would we be born into this current time, if we were just meant to live *free-love, live-off the land* kinda lives? Simple lives, with no career or materialistic growth and no economic self-betterment? If that is how we were meant to live and who we were meant to be, why would we not just have been born into that world?"

Viyan listened thoughtfully to what Zayne argued.

"Talk about philosophical!" he proclaimed.

What Zayne had said made so much of sense and it was just what Viyan was hoping to hear. What if it was just a coincidence that he and Samara had the same dream? He never believed in this sort of thing anyway. Well in the movies maybe, it was plausible there. But this was real life and there was a definitive line between the two. His reality was his current life, how could it be anything else? There was never any other inclining to an alternate truth his entire existence, at least up to now. His life was going pretty well, and it was all on track. He had plans for his future and saving the World was never part of it. The dream was his mind creating a story from what Samara told him. *Coincidence and nothing more!* And that was that!

Chapter Three

The Reveal

The next morning their mum sent a message to the family chat group,

> *'Hey kids. Dad and I need to talk to you. Can you be home early from work? I am cancelling my meetings for the afternoon.'*

Their mum was a psychologist and ran her own practice and their dad was a marketing specialist in a global company.

Samara asked if everything was ok.

Their mum texted back, *'Just a family meeting, no need to panic'.*

Viyan confirmed that they could be home at 4 p.m.

'Great, I'll make us an early dinner'.

On the car ride home they wondered what could be so important, their parents never did this sort of thing. They've never had a family emergency like this before.

"Do you think someone died?!" Samara asked as she turned to look at Viyan.

"Can't be. If it was so important, they would have come to work to tell us."

When they got home, their mum had cooked up a storm; roast chicken and roasted vegetables, baby potatoes and mushroom sauce, and garlic bread.

"Ok, now I know it's serious!" Samara exclaimed at the sight of all the food.

"It is! There is even pecan pie and ice cream for dessert!" Mum replied.

As they sat down at the table she began to plate the food for them, clearly not ready to talk.

"Um, Mom, don't you have something that you want to tell us?" Samara asked.

"Let's eat first. Have a nice family dinner," she replied with a smile.

Viyan and Samara turned to look at each other, deciding to be patient.

"How is work going for you both?" Dad asked, trying to distract them.

"It's going good, and Viyan mentioned something about a promotion."

After dinner, as they helped clear up, they could feel the air becoming tense, knowing that it was time to talk. The suspense had created an awkwardness among them.

"Why don't you all go into the lounge, and I will bring in the dessert," their mum suggested.

As they made their way to the other room Samara whispered to Viyan, "I spent the whole dinner trying to figure out if it's to do with me but it's still the summer break and I haven't gone anywhere apart from work. I couldn't have done anything wrong!"

"This tension even has me stressed out, I'm beginning to think that I did something," Viyan whispered back.

"Unless …" Samara raised her eyes to the ceiling as she concluded her deduction. "… someone at work complained about something. Did you complain?!" she threateningly asked Viyan.

Their mum entered the living room with the dessert and handed a bowl to each of them.

"Oh, my goodness, when last did I eat pecan nut pie!" Samara remarked excitedly as she sniffed the hot dessert. "Yum!" she exclaimed.

Their mum left her dessert on the coffee table and sat next to their dad. Feeling uneasy, she shuffled a bit to get comfortable. Looking at the two of them, she sighed. "This is rather difficult, and I really don't know how to say this or even where to start."

They both stopped eating.

"You are starting to worry me now Mom," Samara said anxiously.

"Oh-kay!" their mother exclaimed as she took in a deep breath and exhaled. "There is something that Dad and I need to tell you, something that we have been protecting you from. A secret that we've kept – an overwhelmingly difficult secret - since the two of you were born."

She paused to look at their dad.

"I will start from the very beginning. You need to learn the full story."

"You both know that Dad and I met at university while we were studying. We were young, not even 20. But when we met, we immediately fell in love, there was an inexplicable spark that ignited when we saw each other." Their parents lovingly looked at each other.

"A spark that has since not gone off," she continued as she clutched her husband's hand.

"The spark in me is about to get grossed out," Samara said as she pulled a gagging face.

Their mum gave them the backstory of how the two met. A story that they had heard many times before, but this time, they actually listened.

Their dad studied Anthropology with a minor in Mythological Studies at university. He was not your typical student. As a matter of fact, their parents were both very different from the crowd. Even when they met, it was clear that the two of them were destined to be together. They were carefree students but their relationship was often tested. They put it down to the motions of being in love, however it was so much more than that. Although they did not know it at the time, there were always forces that were trying to keep them apart. Nevertheless, through everything they always gravitated toward each other, as if they were meant to be, confirming that their love was *written in the stars*.

"There is something that we have kept from you both. When Dad and I eventually got married, I began to get visions and strange dreams."

Samara got up from her chair to sit next to Viyan. Their mum assumed that they thought she was lying. "Look, this may all sound strange and far-fetched to you both, even crazy, like I am making this up," she said trying to convince them. "But believe me, I am not."

They were both quiet, but Samara slowly shook her head to acknowledge what their mum was saying and so she continued with her story.

"I began to randomly dream about a particular goddess. They were very vivid dreams. The first time I dreamt of Her, I found myself in a beautiful field filled with the most gorgeous coloured flowers. I can even remember the aroma. We walked in the field up to an apple tree. She picked off a juicy red apple and handed it to me to eat. Once I did, She began to talk."

Viyan nudged Samara to confirm what he had told her the day before.

"The Goddess told me that Dad and I were destined to meet. Our love was that of fairytales and it was that love which would create and bring into this world special individuals. The Goddess said that I would have two children, a boy and a girl and that they both would be the chosen ones."

Their mum shook her head and gave a little nervous laugh. "Crazy right!? I mean, saying it out aloud after all these years and it still sounds preposterous." She paused, "I remembered every detail as if it was an actual conversation, but I thought that it was just a bizarre dream and didn't make too much of it. I did not tell anyone, not even Dad. The dream kept crossing my mind, as though I had had a strange encounter with someone. Eventually I just moved on and forgot about the Goddess. Until she came to me again."

"I was about eight months pregnant with Viyan and at that point I would nap at any chance I got. The Goddess visited me in one of my dreams and explained that my son would have *a knowing* and that he would be caring and protective. She told me to name him *Love* because that is what he would be. This was a ridiculous gesture. There were so many names I had picked, and *Love* was nowhere near my list. I just brushed the incident off because I had other things to focus on." She smiled at Viyan.

"But then that same week I had a dream," their dad interrupted. "For the first time I dreamt of the Goddess, not knowing that She had visited Mom. She also appeared very vividly in my dreams and led me to the apple tree Mom spoke of. As I sat under the tree, a snake hanging from one of the branches lowered itself to eye level and looked directly at me. I was not afraid, instead, I felt calm when I looked into its eyes. After I bit into the apple given to me, She explained that there were forces that tried to keep us apart but that our love was strong and would create the ones who would one day save the Earth."

He paused a bit.

"It was all so strange, I mean I love comics and superheroes, but my imagination could not have conjured that up. I told Mom about the dream and she told me of hers. *There was no way that both of us having the same dream could have been a coincidence!*"

Again, he paused.

"I can remember it still so clearly. What stunned us the most was that the Goddess had told me to name you Viyan and when we looked up the meaning of the name, we found two; '*Special Knowledge*' in Sanskrit and '*Love*' in Kurdish.

"And I felt an inexplicable pull toward the name *Varunesh*, which means '*Lord of Water*', because you used to swim in my tummy when I was pregnant," his mum added to the story.

Viyan felt a lump in his throat. He had never asked his parents what his name had meant but here they were, confirming what he was told in his dream. He moved around in his seat, feeling all of a sudden uncomfortable.

"Ok! How long have you guys been thinking up this?" he asked. "There is no way this really happened!"

He was testing them; they must have found out about the dream he had. Their parents used to often prank them when they were younger, this had to have been one of their tricks.

Viyan turned to Samara, "YOU TOLD THEM, DIDN'T YOU?" he accused. "And then you guys came up with this as a joke."

Why am I getting so angry? he thought to himself as his heart began to beat faster.

"I promise I didn't!" Samara said in defence. "This is all so crazy for me too."

"Did you two have a dream as well?" their mother asked softly, concerned.

They both looked at each other and then Viyan began to explain how they had both dreamt of the Goddess and that similarities had occurred in their dreams as well. Samara added that the Goddess told them both that they were destined to save the Earth. They had no idea how they were supposed to, only that they would know when the time came.

"Do you have any idea?" Samara asked her parents.

"We were also only told that you two would one day save the World. Nothing more than that," their mum replied in a lowered tone.

Durga visited again just before Samara was born. The Goddess appeared once more in her mum's dream. She gave Samara her name, which means, *'Guardian or Protected by God'* in Arabic and Hebrew and *Saranya* which means *'Giver of Refuge and Defender'* in Sanskrit. Durga elaborated on the meanings and explained that their names were very important in expressing who they would become and what they would do. *Their names would ultimately define them.*

"That is why when I felt drawn to the name *Xaria*, meaning *Gift of Love,* I named you that in secret," their mum said as she looked at Samara. "You both are my whole heart and I wanted you to always be protected by my love," she said with a lump in her throat and tears in her eyes.

Their dad completed the story, "Durga didn't visit again till Samara was almost three. She stressed that you would need to be kept safe because there would be constant threats against your wellbeing. It was known that two siblings born in Africa would be the saviours and so forces would always be trying to prevent you from fulfilling your destiny."

They had been a close-knit family, happy in their community in Johannesburg, South Africa. But certain happenings made their parents question their safety, so they decided that if the prophecy was true, it would be best if they relocated to protect their children. A job opportunity allowed their dad to transfer and he was able to move the family to San Francisco in America. Their parents knew that the day would eventually come when their children would have to venture on their journey, but they decided to keep the truth from Viyan and Samara for as long as they could.

Within a few months of moving to America, the Goddess appeared for the last time. To keep their location hidden, it was best that She no longer kept in contact. But before She parted, She reminded them that the day would come when they would have to face their truth. Life resumed but as their children grew, Viyan and Samara's parents knew that they would not be able to shelter them forever. For their safety, the family strategically relocated once again, this time to Florida in America. Florida was a busy tourist state and they hoped that it would throw off any direct linkage to the siblings. Also, their parents had hoped that it was all just a crazy, mad experience and that by escaping their past, they could forget it.

"Ok, so if this is all true, why did you hide it from us?" Samara asked.

"Look, Dad and I were not sure if it was true and with time we wondered if it had even happened. It took us a long time to adjust to normalcy and we kept waiting for Durga to visit us again, but She never did … until now that is."

"Is this the reason that we were never really religious?" Samara asked.

"We decided to live non-religious lives so that you two would not have any inclination to your destiny. We thought that it would be best for you to not know anything and to discover your own path," their mother answered.

"I did wonder why a Hindu goddess would come to us," Samara said. "If anything, we know more about *Greek mythology than Hindu mythology.*"

"How did you know who it was that came to you in your dreams then?" her mum asked.

"Google!" Samara exclaimed with a nod.

There was silence for a little while and then their mother expressed how she had hoped that it was merely a misunderstanding.

"After all these years, the Goddess visited me again last night. She said that it was time for destiny to be fulfilled and that you are both ready to carry out what was written for you.

This is the reason why we are telling you now. We don't have a choice anymore." She began to tear up.

"I am not ready! I thought that it was a mistake. I never thought I had to let you do this. I am not even sure what *this* is," she continued.

"Well neither do we," Samara added. "We also don't know if any of what is happening is real."

They sat in silence for a while. Eerily the speaker in the living area switched on automatically and *Listen* by Beyonce began to play. The words echoed in the silence …

'Listen to the sound from deep within, it's only beginning to find release. Oh, the time has come for my dreams to be heard, they will not be pushed aside or turned.'

Then, midway through the song, the volume lowered. They looked at each other. That was awfully strange. The confusion was broken by a commotion outside followed by a scratch at the door.

"I am not going to look!" Samara said nervously as she moved back into her chair.

Their dad walked up to the window to check who was there but he could not see anything. He opened the front door. To his surprise, on the porch stood a huge, sandy brown Chow-Chow. Samara ran to look when their dad said, "Oh hi there fella!"

"Oh my gosh! He looks like a little lion!" Samara shouted.

The dog walked up to Samara and licked her arm. He then moved over to Viyan to sniff him. Viyan bent to pat the dog and noticed that he had a collar with an inscription on it. It read, *Shamanic Secret Keepers.*

"That's a strange name for a dog!" Samara stated, confused.

Viyan, in the meanwhile, instinctively went on to his phone to look for the *Shamanic People*.

"I think we need to find this tribe," he said as he showed them the image. And they are right next door, in Georgia. I feel that they will have answers for us."

Without hesitation, he knew that they needed to find the tribe. He couldn't explain how he knew because it was so unconscious. *How did I know they are a tribe and that they would have the answers that we need?* he thought to himself. *What is happening to me?*

They went silent for a bit, absorbing all the information. It had become clear that *this,* was all real.

Their mum broke the tension, "Well, it has been a lot for one night. Let's just go to bed and take a fresh revisit in the morning. *Ok?*"

"I take it that the dog is staying?" Viyan asked as he gave him a pat on the head. "I'll take him up to bed with me. Night everyone."

That night Samara dreamt of Durga. The Goddess explained that it was becoming risky for her to contact Samara, so that visit would be the last till it was safe again. As the time drew closer for their mission, it became increasingly dangerous and was no longer secure for both Samara and Viyan. The Goddess told her that everything would fall into place once they found the tribe but that she needed to trust herself and to trust Viyan. This was the most important thing for her to do – to trust her intuition.

Samara expressed her uncertainty. "This is all still so strange, and it does not make any sense. I just went along as it was happening but now that the time draws near, as you say, I feel so much pressure. Why won't you tell me what this mission is and why won't you just tell me what we need to do?"

The Goddess felt Samara's anxiety and tried to calm her down.

"The reason that I cannot tell you what your mission is, is because I do not want to influence you by explaining any details or implications. I cannot tell you the future because it could be altered, and it needs to take its natural course without any influence. I want you to start the journey on your own, discover the process and make your own decisions from there. The people you will meet on your journey know what the mission is and know where you need to go. It will all seem strange and unrealistic, but you must just remember to believe."

Samara nodded, accepting what Durga explained.

"*Are you God?*" she asked arbitrarily. "I've watched *Bruce Almighty* and with all that has happened, you could very well be."

"Oh, Samara! Your humour and innocence are what I have always loved about you."

The Goddess entertained her question, "I am not God, there is no one true God. I was created as a form of God; as a representation. You were created in that image, in human form. Even your name *Saranya* is a name given to me to understand one of my forms, that of *defender*. Simply a visual interpretation for humans to connect to."

The Goddess tried to simplify it. "There is so much more to reality that humans are unaware of. That is why the gods cannot come to Earth, it is too complicated to do so. Since God can never come to Earth, you will represent me here as *Defender* and *Protector*."

She told Samara that because it was not safe to visit her anymore, even in her dreams, She would send forms and messages where She could, but the Goddess had to stay away as it would compromise everything. Once they found the tribe, things would become clearer.

"Oh, and don't forget to take Simha with you."

"*Simha*?" Samara questioned.

"The dog," Durga said with a smile.

Before the Goddess faded away, she outstretched her arms to reveal eight in total; each concealing an artefact.

"These weapons will protect you, they will help you in your fight to destroy Rahu!"

The Goddess vanished and Samara woke in a sweat.

"Where am I supposed to get those weapons from? And what is a *Rahu*?" she asked aloud.

The next morning the family found each other in the kitchen. It took a few moments of silence before they began to discuss what their next moves were, each one thinking to themselves how crazy it all was. Samara was the last to arrive. She poured herself a cup of coffee.

"So … Durga came to me again last night. She said that it was the last time that I would see Her because it's no longer safe. She told me that once we found the tribe, everything would fall into place and that we would figure out our mission from there."

"We know!" Viyan cut her off. "We've just been waiting for you to make an appearance so that we could get started."

It could not be a strange, coincidental, dream if all of them saw the same thing, so they decided to do what they were guided to; to find the Shamanic people. And even if it was just a coincidence, at least they could spend some family time on a road trip.

Viyan and Samara sat to map out where they needed to go and also what they needed, or at least thought they would need for the journey ahead. Their mum had packed snacks, pillows and throws into the car. She tried to distract herself from the reality of what was happening by preparing for the journey. "We're all packed! As soon as you guys are ready, we can hit the road," she declared.

The family was pulling out of the driveway when Samara yelled, "*Stop!* We forgot something!"

She ran into the house and came back out with Simha and a bowl. "Being responsible for something else is surely going to take some getting used to," she proclaimed as she jumped back into the car.

Chapter Four

The Shamanic People

The drive was long and they had to stop ever so often to let Simha out to stretch his legs. Viyan swapped seats with his dad at one of the stops. He drove the rest of the way while the others napped. Abruptly, he braked hard and the immediate stop woke everyone up.

"What!? What happened?" Samara asked in shock. "Are we there yet?"

They had reached an enclosure of trees which caused a blockage.

"Something tells me that we are going to need to park here and walk the rest of the way." They followed Viyan's instinct and parked the car.

The sun was setting but luckily their mum had packed some flashlights. She grabbed a backpack from the car which had some outdoor essentials. Their mum was always prepared, as mums usually are. But she was a bit of a perfectionist and perhaps it was where Viyan got his trait from.

Viyan felt something pull him in the direction that they needed to head toward and Simha confirmed this by almost leading Samara in that direction. There was only silence as they walked, individually contemplating if they were making a mistake, if they were being foolish in their search. But no one admitted their reservations. They walked the way without a word spoken, only following Simha's guidance. Each was stuck in their own head. Finally, they spotted a compound in the distance and jointly felt a sense of relief at the find.

As they approached the village, they could make out the dwellings of the inhabitants; tipi-like huts. The sun had now set but the bright night sky lit the surroundings. Some of the villagers could be seen milling about the tents. They walked over to meet the family, unalarmed by their visitors. The villagers were dressed in traditional Native American tribal clothing. Tan-coloured clothes with bits of coloured patterns, made from animal skin and trimmed with fur accents. Their jewellery was fashioned out of feathers, animal teeth and claws. Some of the ladies wore headpieces with matching bracelets and necklaces made of flowers. The first impression of the village was that it was untouched, preserved for decades.

Samara and Viyan proceeded to meet the tribe while their parents followed. One of the males approached them and without saying anything, led them to what seemed like the largest tent in the middle of the compound. Some of the members followed them inside. All the while, no one saying anything to them. The villagers either welcomed visitors very often or were expecting the family's arrival. Viyan introduced himself and then his family, but no one responded to him, they just smiled and nodded as if they did not understand. One of the tribesmen left the tent and then there was complete silence. An elderly lady gestured for them to sit on the mats arranged out on the floor. A few minutes later, although it seemed much longer in all of the silence, the hut's door flapped open and in walked an older man. He seemed to be the tribe-leader as his headpiece stood out from all the others.

The man sat down on a mat in front of them and looked at Samara. He reached out his hand, palm side up, gesturing that she give him hers. Samara placed out her left hand. The old man shook his head and pointed to the other hand. Samara then placed her right palm on his. The man turned it over so that her palm faced upward. He looked at her hand and ran a finger over the strawberry-coloured heart-shaped birthmark on the bottom left-hand corner of her palm, near her wrist. The man looked back up at her and smiled. He began to speak in English.

"We have been waiting for you," he said. "Many, many years. We have been guarding the secret for all this time, waiting for the day that you would come for us to reveal it." The man excitedly clapped his hands once together.

Samara always thought that the birthmark was quite odd. It never really bothered her, but it was a strange place for a birthmark. As a little girl, she would pretend that it was a lock and that one day she would find the key that fit it. That day had come.

Samara looked at Viyan and then back at the leader.

"Soooooo, you know who we are then?"

He smiled at her, "We have been waiting for you, we knew that you would be coming but we just did not know exactly when." The Chief had a passive tone.

"How do you know that we are the ones you were waiting for?" Viyan asked, making sure that these were indeed the Shamanic people they were searching for.

"Our village is protected; it is hidden from other humans. You can only find it if you are meant to. You most certainly are the ones we have been waiting for."

"But it was just there in the middle of the forest for anyone to access. Actually, we parked our car not too far away from here," Viyan said gesturing in the direction. He tried to stress that the village was not as invisible as the Chief seemed to believe, it was rather quite obvious. Anyone could find it.

"Yes, but something guided you here, correct?" he asked softly.

"I intuitively knew to come this way," Viyan agreed reluctantly, still not understanding what the man was trying to prove.

He could not see it from where he stood but an aerial view would show a clearing in the middle of the forest. A circular grassy path, about three kilometres in diameter, sat in the middle of the forest. Above this clearing was a mirror-like protective dome that made it look as if the forest continued with no interruption. Beneath this dome sat the home of the tribe; grasslands occupied by a village of tipis and livestock all belonging to the Shamanic People. This is what the Chief was trying to explain; that unless you were meant to see the reservation, it would simply look like a continuous forest.

"This village is not visible to everyone, and you would not be drawn to come here unless you were supposed to. The only ones that are guided to come to the village are tribesmen or *Guardians*."

"*What are Guardians?*" Samara asked.

The Chief smiled a hearty smile as though she had asked the perfect question. "*You are!*"

He stood up to walk to the opposite end of the pit that they all had their backs toward. The family turned around to face the pit as he lit a fire in it and began to tell them a story.

The fire burned low at first and then began to grow. While the Chief told the story the flames began to dance as if they were visually re-enacting his words. They watched the flames as the Chief narrated. His voice was deep and slow as he told them the history of his tribe and of Humans.

"When the Earth came to be She was an infant planet, young compared to all of those already orbiting in the galaxy. She lived in harmony with other creatures for millions of years as she developed."

The flames formed the silhouettes of many creatures, some familiar and most not. An image of the Earth was seen in the middle of the fire and visuals of creatures such as dinosaurs and mammoths along strange looking beings burned in and out alongside the Earth.

The Chief continued, "Eventually the *human* form was created. They were different to the creatures that already roamed the planet. Although they were the youngest species, they were one of the most intelligent. *Man* was meant to inhabit Earth and create and cultivate a world for all the Earth's creatures to grow in. Man's form was a new creation to the Universe and to guide this new creation the older living beings from other more mature planets who had already been sent to Earth, were assigned to guard Earth and to guide Man on their journey. These beings were to live in harmony with Man and the Earth. They kept to the task asked of them but the human species being young and naïve did not. With time, Man became full of ego and materialism and began to want more." The Chief paused as he watched the fire depict the creation of the Cosmos.

"*The Guardians* were those creatures sent to guide Man and guard the Earth. The Shamanic People were human in form but were tasked to be part of the Guardians. They had a deep knowledge about themselves and had a different understanding of the World compared to the rest of humanity. They were given the gift of *natural healing* and *natural magic,* and they used these gifts to help Man learn and grow as a species."

The Chief explained what Durga had introduced to Samara – that humans lived initially like the Shamanic people, off the Earth and in large familial communities. They lived in harmony with the Earth and did not harm Her in any way as she nourished and sustained their lives. But, with time Man became influenced by greed and power. Man, who once lived together with the other creatures, began to see themselves as different from the others on Earth. Because Man was the youngest creation, they felt that they were superior to others. Driven by their ego, they began to seek new lands, separate from the creatures sent to guide them. Eventually, as Man found differences among each other, they divided themselves into different tribes. Disagreements and egocentric ideas led to separation as more and more tribes were formed, each wanting to be more powerful than the next. Power-hungry, leaders of these tribes began to create rivalries with each other.

The flames swelled as they showed how man towered over the other creatures. The Chief's voice became harsher, "The creatures sent to protect the Earth were old and wise and knew how other planets were destroyed through greed and power. They wanted to maintain peace and protect the Earth as they were asked to. But Man, with hate in their eyes, began to see these creatures as threats to their power and slowly Man turned on them."

The flames began to grow intensely as they showed how the men began to fight. They depicted men fighting the creatures that they lived among and then as these creatures vanished within the flames, they showed how the men began to fight each other. The flames displayed war and destruction as Man was revealed as murderous - violently destroying the Earth.

The group focused on the dramatic flames as the Chief continued.

He unpacked the Guardians' descent, explaining that while they were missioned to protect Earth and to guide Man, when the time came to protect themselves, they chose rather to not fight. Even though they were given many talents and powers that would have ensured their victory, they chose peace instead. It was because of this pacifism that they went into hiding.

Man began to separate from each other forming tribes across the continents. To keep future generations away from the other tribes and to maintain their tribal power, the leaders began to create rivalries. Ensuring that the younger generations would not befriend the Guardians, tales that depicted them as evil and even deadly were created. These fallacies became folklore and later with time, they became worldwide myths. As the years passed, the tribes forgot their heritage and eventually Man evolved to where they are today. Still driven by power and greed, now more than ever, Man continues to increasingly create hierarchies and differences amongst the human race.

Controlled by personal selfish gain, Man forgot their history and their purpose.

In the chaos, the Shamanic People made it their mission to maintain the Earth and protect the legacy of the Guardians. They knew of the threat that would one day befall Earth and this was the reason why their people did not enter mainstream society. The Chief's voice lowered in tone as the fire became still. "To this day, many tribes have decided to remain untouched by society so that they can preserve the Earth. We, however, are the only tribe that holds the secret to the location of all the Guardians. Many moons ago, my ancestors accepted the task to be the *Secret Keepers*. When we separated from the other Guardians, my people made the decision to continue living where we had settled and not to go into hiding like the others had. By maintaining our ways we were hopeful that the Earth could return to what She once was."

"But were you not concerned about being at risk, concerned about being vulnerable to threats for the secret that you keep?" Viyan asked, consumed by the story but at the same time trying to be realistic about the Chief's telling.

"Sometimes we cannot see what is in plain sight," the Chief answered.

"We are also protected. There have been many threats to my people over the years, but we would not have accepted our task without any protection. Our Shamanic tribe and our natural practices may be known, but Man does not know of us as *Secret Keepers*. Our tribe was once visible to educate others on nature and healing but we have had to protect ourselves from the outside world now that the mission will commence. Those that would be a threat to us, cannot find us. You found us because you were meant to."

"You say that you are the Secret Keepers. What deep, dark, mysterious secrets do you keep?" Samara asked, intrigued by the name.

For generations the tribe protected the secret of who all the Guardians were, and it was finally time to unveil them to Viyan and Samara. The Chief called his granddaughter to bring forth the scroll that bore all the sacred information. She was standing in the crowd that had gathered in the tipi. Viyan's heart skipped a beat when he saw her. She was breathtaking. Tall with golden-brown skin, mesmerizing hazel-coloured eyes and full lips. Her hair was long and braided into two plaits, with a feathered headpiece over the plaits. Gracefully she walked, upright in posture, as she slowly brought forward a small wooden chest which housed the scroll.

The chest looked deceivingly unsecured, but the Chief had to perform a ritual before he could open it. He took the chest and laid it next to the fire, onto a mat made from small, thin tree branches woven together. Alongside the chest, he placed a small vessel containing water from the nearby lake and he removed a feather from his headpiece which he rested beside the water. He placed the elements around the chest; *Earth, fire, water and the feather which represented air.* Before picking up the chest he closed his eyes and silently prayed. He raised the vial of water with one hand and then picked up some earth, combined with the feather, with the other. He threw the water into the fire and blew these materials to combine with the water. As the elements merged with the life from his breath, the fire blazed. The Chief stood with the box in both hands when the flames jumped out from the fire pit to encircle the chest. As the flames surrounded the chest, the Chief softly uttered an incantation. When he was done, the flames receded and the Chief pulled the chest toward him as it opened on its own.

The Chief unrolled the sacred scroll and showed it to Viyan and Samara. While the scroll glowed brightly, a closer view revealed that it was blank. As he straightened it out, the Chief explained that the scroll had a protection spell placed upon it and that the words could not be seen by just anyone. The scroll held the names of the Guardians and one by one the Chief began to reveal who they were. "We, the Shamanic Tribe are one of the Guardians of Earth, then there are the two of you," the Chief highlighted before unveiling the rest.

"For this mission, eight of the Earth's Guardians have been purposefully chosen; some of us tribes, some of us individuals. We are scattered across the Earth and it is you that must find the rest and bring them together."

Samara turned to look at Viyan, both dumbfounded by who the Guardians were. Viyan turned to the Chief, "These are mythological creatures known throughout the world. We have heard of them and read accounts of people claiming to have seen them, but do they really exist?"

"Yes, they do, and they have been around for millennia. They have just been in hiding because of their history with Man. They hid to protect the Earth, but they still very much do exist."

"Ok, so I understand that it is our destiny to save the Earth but what exactly do we need to save Her from?" Samara asked as the question ran through her mind. "What is this *threat* against Her?"

"Ever since the Earth was created, there were those that did not agree with the plan for Her. As with everything, there is *good and bad, positive and negative*; this is the natural balance. Humans were created in this balance, in this neutrality. And we were initially good in our being but with an individual choice to maintain this nature or not. Naturally, as time passed, temptation came about. *The Threat* that you need to protect the Earth from is the *negative*, the dark energy known as *Rahu.*"

"*Rahu!*" Samara yelped, remembering the last thing that Durga had said to her.

The Chief looked at her confused and then continued, "Man was created to have basic good intentions and was given everything needed to live a wholesome, joyous life on Earth. The objective was that humans would live a life on Earth where their souls would learn lessons and ultimately become enlightened. Earth was supposed to be a training ground where our spirits would come to experience life and in so doing, learn soul lessons amongst other souls."

"Oh my gosh, I just had a realisation!" Samara exclaimed, cutting the Chief off again through his explanation. She turned to Viyan.

"It's like Jumanji Next Level!" she declared excitedly as she grabbed his hand. Everything was suddenly making complete sense. "You know how they come into the game with three lives but then when they die, they come back as another character to learn a different lesson and to learn how to use their different talents. That's what life and reincarnation is! We come back as other people to have a different experience of the World and to learn new lessons."

Viyan thought about her analysis, it was a rather insightful deduction.

"It's like all the explanations were there in the movie, but we just didn't see it!" Samara epiphanised, gesturing with her hands before relaxing her hyped up posture.

They both looked back at the Chief who was waiting for them to finish.

"She just equated life to a game," Viyan explained to the Chief.

"That is a very good analogy," the Chief confirmed.

"We are all just pawns in a game, overcoming obstacles and challenges to get to the finish line, but most importantly, learning and growing along the way. That is what the plan for humans was, but the negative energy balance did not agree with this. This negative force believed that Man would be consumed by their ego and thus was ultimately negative in nature, and so believed that we should be created in this form. As a compromise, the decision was that Man would be given free will to decide who they would be."

The Chief paused to think before explaining to them, "You need to remember that the Devil and God are not physical forms but Man's creation to decipher difference and to give structure to these elements. They are simply good and bad energy – the duality, the opposite – and one cannot exist without the other. And the way we believe them to look are the forms in which they appear to us."

"Or the way that we imagine them to look because we can understand them better when we have a physical form to relate to," Samara added, remembering her conversation with Durga.

The Chief nodded in agreement.

"The problem with bad energy is that it can consume the good, and just like good energy, it can also grow. So, while it can be harmless in its infancy and necessary to decipher the element of good, if left to spread it can become, even unintentionally, destructive."

He paused once more before continuing.

"As with every creation, the Creator loved the human species and did not want them to be influenced. So, a protective field was placed around the Earth to inhibit any negative influence and to guarantee that Man would decide their path for themselves. This protective force is known scientifically as the o*zone layer*. However, it not only protects the Earth from the sun but from external negative threats as well. As time went on, sadly Man did indeed begin to gravitate to a more negative energy as a collective. Negative energy can easily influence and eventually transform neutral or good energy. This negative energy impacted the Earth and the protective ozone and as a result, it became increasingly thin. It is now only a matter of time before it disappears altogether and leaves the Earth unprotected from all negative threats."

Viyan smiled nervously as he nodded, trying to comprehend what he had learnt. "Ok, let me try to understand this," Samara said waving her hands around as she spoke. "Viyan and I need to find all the Guardians of Earth and bring them together so that they can repair the ozone layer? And if we do not, then the layer will disappear, and this will allow the negative forces to come through and destroy Earth and all humans?"

"In summary, yes," the Chief agreed.

"The negative energy will not directly destroy Earth, but it will influence negative thinking and selfishness and that will consume all the positive energy within Man. This will affect, and in time kill, the Earth and thus Man too. Everything is created in a delicate balance and ultimately connected. As the ozone layer increasingly thinned with time, more negative influences were able to come to Earth. You two need to stop Rahu, and the negative forces that will eventually consume the remaining positive energy on Earth, and help restore the balance."

Viyan wiped his sweaty palms on his pants and exhaled a few deep breaths. "But this is not something for the two of us! I mean I have a job to get back to and I have a big responsibility … I mean this is not the plan … what about my friends?"

He felt anxious as his mind raced. "Na, this can't be real. It does not make any sense. This is like the plot of any superhero movie where the *everyday Joe* miraculously becomes a hero. Spiderman, Shazam, Hulk, She-hulk … every superhero. But they all have powers to help … and we don't. Nope, none of this is real!"

Flustered, he stood up and left the tent.

His mum was about to follow after him when his dad held her hand to stop her. Viyan needed some space.

Not affected by Viyan leaving, as if he had expected it, the Chief continued talking to Samara. "I think you can start your journey tomorrow, now that you have learnt your mission. My granddaughter, Catori, will accompany you. Just like you, she has been training for this. It is her destiny to guide you."

Samara turned to look at Catori and gave her a warm smile. Catori, with her perfect posture, stared at Samara before giving her a quick bow of the head in return. Samara turned back to look at the Chief and nodded in agreement. She then left the tent to check up on Viyan who she found outside, looking into the distant sky. She slowly walked up to him, and side by side they stared into the distance.

The moon lit the night sky. The stars shone so brightly and clearly, resembling sparkling diamonds twinkling high above. The constellations could be mapped out so perfectly. A sight that they had never seen before. The pollution-free environment provided a viewing so faultless that it was like looking at the night sky a thousand years ago.

Samara exhaled deeply, "I know you don't believe any of this, but I do. I can't explain it, I just do. It's a feeling, a sense of purpose. It sounds ridiculous, I know! But I just believe it … it feels like everything is finally starting to make sense for me and I don't doubt any of it."

She turned to look at him.

"I believe that I am destined to do this … but I can't do it without you."

There was silence.

"How long is going to take? I have to get back to my studies after the summer break." He couldn't help it, he would do anything for his sister, even if it was the most outrageous notion possible.

Samara smiled. "It can't take longer than that, I have school too you know. And it's an important year for me, I have a few decisions to make when I get back."

Their parents came out to join them.

"Mom, can you please let my office know that there is an emergency and that I won't be coming in for a few weeks," Viyan asked.

"I know this is against your policy and I am not sure what you're gonna say but I think you're going to have to lie for us," Samara winked.

"Let the boys know too will ya? Zayne is going to have to find a way to get to work. And don't forget to feed Sushi! And I have a stack of books I was going to donate this weekend. Oh, and I was supposed to tutor that kid for the rest of the summer and help the other one with the drums …"

His dad placed his hand on Viyan's shoulder, calming him down.

"Relax. Your fish will be fine … everything will be fine. We will handle things at home. I got this!" He winked at him and nodded his head as if to say, *it's going to be all right.*

While their parents were there with them this entire time, they knew that they had to go on their journey alone. Their parents knew this too; at the back of their minds, they always carried with them the knowing that the time would come for their children to walk their own path. Their mum tried as best to contain herself, but she couldn't stop a few tears from falling. She hugged and kissed them. She always knew that this moment would come, it was a given from the moment that they were born. But it didn't mean that this was any easier.

"We are so, so proud of you. And it is difficult, but we are proud of the path that is about to unfold for you. Always remember that we are your biggest fans, and we believe so strongly in you both."

She held each of their hands in hers.

"I am so sorry that we didn't tell you sooner, it is only because I wanted to protect you for as long as I could. But this destiny would not have chosen you if you were not meant for it. You will succeed! And our love will be supporting you every step of the way."

Barely able to sleep, they awoke at sunrise and started preparing for the journey ahead. The tribespeople had packed food, milk, water and some necessities for the road.

"No coffee then?" Samara asked as she accepted the food.

Their mum hugged and kissed them both.

"I am so proud of you both, you have no idea!" she said holding on to them tightly. Turning to their dad, she held him, unable to watch her kids leave.

"We love you too, so, so much," Samara whispered back to her mum and then turned away so as not to show how emotional she was.

"Are we going in our car?" Viyan asked.

"This journey requires you to go back to nature, way back," the Chief responded with a smile. The tribesmen brought forward a horse for each of them to journey on. Their dad walked up to Viyan. "My credit card and some cash. Looks like you are going to need it!" he said as he hugged them both.

"Mom, I think you are going to need to take Simha back with you," Samara looked sadly at the dog as she spoke.

"No!" the Chief interrupted. "It is imperative that the dog goes with you. But he cannot go with you where you will be going next."

The Chief paused to think before finishing.

"Leave him with us, we will get him to you when you need him."

Samara was confused by the Chief's suggestion, but she did not say anything in return. *How could a dog be imperative for the journey? Is he a Guardian?* she thought to herself.

They mounted their horses and rode off. As they were making their way across the reservation, Samara noticed that on the saddle of Catori's horse was a bow and a quiver with arrows. She remembered seeing a bow in Durga's hand in her last vision. Samara felt that a piece was being fit into the puzzle. She smiled as she galloped off, ready for the journey and confident that she had made the right decision - that this was what she was meant to do. She was answering the call of her destiny.

The Adventure Begins

They headed in a northerly direction. Viyan and Samara both trailed behind Catori without any conversation. With a raise of her eyes and a nod of her head in Catori's direction, Samara motioned for Viyan to talk to her. Catori turned around but Viyan just looked at her and smiled.

"I bet you are wondering if I speak," she said in perfect English.

"I do," she continued.

Viyan found that he could not say anything in response. He just continued to smile. Realising that he was shy, Samara replied instead, "Well, that's a relief! Else this mission would have encountered its first problem. Communication is key you know."

Catori remained emotionless as the two rode up next to her.

"I did wonder, but I did not want to ask. How is it that your grandfather spoke such excellent English, even though you all are so withdrawn from the rest of society?"

"Yes, we have lived separately from others, but it was only so that we could preserve our ways and keep our mission sacred. Nevertheless, we had to know what was happening in the world around us to be aware of all the changes. Some of our tribe's people left to learn the ways of the World and came back to teach us. My grandfather was one of these tribesmen. He went out to study the greater society and learnt to speak English, among other languages. When he returned, he continued his learnings within the tribe and eventually assumed his role as Chief."

"Wow, that is … progressive," Samara responded.

Catori's tone was serious and impassive, "Our ancestors believed that the Chiefs of the tribe should venture out into the wider world so that they would become better leaders if they knew what they were protecting the tribe from. And similarly, my grandfather believed that I follow the same path. I had left the tribe with my parents and some others for a few years when I was younger. I got to experience the outer world, but because we knew that you would be coming, we had to return home."

There was a short silence before Samara spoke again, "Ok, so what is the plan? Where do we go from here?"

"We need to ride off in a northern direction through the forest. It is going to take a day and a half, depending on how we get on, before we reach our destination. We will need to camp tonight and rest," Catori explained.

"And you're familiar with the journey and what we need for the camp?" Viyan asked softly.

"Ahhh, so you do speak," Catori said to Viyan. "Yes, I am familiar with the forest and know the way, otherwise this is the first time that I too make the full journey."

That night they camped out and Catori made a small fire to heat the food that the tribespeople had packed for them. "I am so glad that we are making this trip in summer, if it were winter, I most probably would have declined," Samara said as she moved closer to warm her hands at the fire.

"Well don't count your lucky stars too soon," Catori responded.

Though still expressionless, it seemed that Catori was warming up to the siblings. Her demeanor, while still perfect in posture, seemed more relaxed.

"What is that supposed to mean?" Samara asked, concerned. "I didn't pack warm. No I'm serious, I hate the cold! You have to tell me."

Catori just smiled at Samara. Viyan joined them as they sat around the fire heating the bread, corn and cooked vegetables.

"She thinks I'm joking," Samara whispered as he sat beside her.

Once they had finished eating, Catori told them that she needed some quiet to figure out what direction they would need to travel from that point onward. "I need to concentrate."

She turned toward the fire and added another log before gathering some sand from the ground. She held the sand in her hand and closed her eyes to meditate. There was complete silence until she threw the handful of sand into the fire. The fire sparked and Catori began to breathe … in and out, slowly but deeply. She raised her hands beside the fire and opened her eyes, just as her grandfather did. The fire began to tell a story, just as it had in the village. They saw themselves and the horses journey across some dry, barren land until they came to a forest. In the fire, they saw a pack of wolves approach them. Then the fire went still. A moment later an image of a little Shamanic girl appeared within the fire. She stood in the centre with the flames blazing around her, but she did not move. Suddenly, she raised her right arm and pointed.

Samara was shocked and gasped, "Hahhh!"

She calmed herself down noticing that she was the only one startled.

"Channeling some *Blaire Witch* vibes there Catori?" she said, straightening up again.

The fire then stilled completely, and Catori uttered calmly, "I know in which direction we have to go."

"Let us get some rest for an early start to tomorrow," she recommended as she unpacked the sleeping bags tied to the horses' saddles.

They placed the bags next to the fire and lay down to sleep.

Tucked in her bag, Samara couldn't sleep. "I want to know more about you and how you felt knowing that you were chosen for this mission. Also, having to return to the tribe after experiencing the real world, I don't know if I could give up comfort to return to living permanently outside."

"Mmm, where do I start!" Catori expressed.

"I lived my whole life in Kakahoyan, we call it Kayah, it is the name of my land, and where I went to school. Our school was not the same as yours. We learnt languages, English and my native tongue, NAfAEAuAsSA but more importantly, we learnt life. Then my family left to venture into the greater world. Since I was little, I always accepted that this was my mission. I knew that I was meant to do something more. So, when we returned to the tribe, as magical as the world out there was, I was happy to be home. And when I did return, I trained harder because I wanted to be the best that I could be. I learnt how to work with Nature and use Her powers. I was taught by my grandfather, the high Chief, and studied natural magic through him." You could tell in her voice and the way that she spoke of her grandfather, that she was very proud of her lineage.

"We still had our people living on the outside and they came back to educate the rest of us on the changes so that we would always be aware of what was transpiring. In our tribe we all had a purpose and even though we may have been tempted to explore the outer world, we focused on our role and the greater good of Man. Apart from the ones who were assigned to ventured out, my tribe has maintained our closeness to Nature over all these many years. While we were given the gift of natural magic and healing, as time moved on, many stopped practicing because it takes commitment to learn and maintain the power."

Catori paused for a bit before continuing.

"You must understand that my people have been around for a very, very long time, it was foreseeable that we would lose our belief eventually. Because of this loss of hope, our people as a society lost the gift. But every high Chief had to continue training to keep the magic alive for the time when it would be needed. And so, I have learnt too because I knew that this day was coming."

"How did you know that the stories were true? That this time would eventually come? Did you not lose some hope too? I mean there have been generations that have passed and the prophecy still didn't come true. How did you know that it was more than just a legend?" Samara asked Catori, making sure for herself that the mission was indeed real.

"I did not know. I guess I just believed that it was. It was a feeling, a trusting that it was all true." Catori validated that the confusion was normal. "Besides, this was not your first life. You have been on Earth before this, and my people knew of your previous life forms. That kept us invested."

"Yesterday your grandfather mentioned that we too have been training for this mission. I was concerned with Viyan leaving the tent, that I didn't ask what he meant."

"It was a prophecy that you would come down to Earth over many lifetimes, to train for this very mission. But this is the first time that you are *on* the mission. This is what you have been living for!"

"But I do not remember anything else besides my current life!" Samara stated in bewilderment.

"I agree," Viyan added.

He had been rather quiet the entire journey. He found himself somewhat introverted in Catori's company. A strange feeling for him because he was normally not a reserved person. In fact, he was usually the confident one, not Samara. Catori's beauty had him tongue-tied. But it was not just her, he also found that he was not himself since the *dream*.

"I do not remember any other lifetimes besides this life as me. This is my only life and I find it hard to grasp that I have lived many lives before. If I did, how do I not know it?" Viyan asked, finding it difficult to make sense of this new path. "I am just going with everything. I find this all hard to understand and honestly the only reason that I am here is because Samara and my parents believe it."

"Give it time," Catori comforted. "You have unexpectedly learnt that something great is being asked of you, it is not easy to accept but it will all fall into place. You'll see." She gave him a warm, assuring smile.

Catori was wise beyond her years and this maturity was carried through in the way she presented herself. As Chief-in-waiting, she could have been groomed to be this way, or perhaps it was simply her personality. Whichever it was, it was evident that her serious manner was beginning to abate.

"I think we should get some sleep, we have to rise early tomorrow," she said, before turning over.

Samara waited some time for Catori to fall asleep before turning over to ask Viyan, "Why did you agree to do this?"

"Because you needed me to," he replied.

"But you don't believe any of this is true. Why would you waste your time on a stupid journey if you think it is going to lead us nowhere?"

"Because you believe that it's true. And even if it's not, at least we will know then, but I would never forgive myself for not supporting you in finding out."

"But you …"

He cut her off. "And I finally know what it's like to feel lost … and it's a horrible feeling."

She turned completely over in her sleeping sack to look at him.

"What do you mean?"

"My life was structured. So far it has always gone according to plan, and I believed that it did because I worked hard. And because I made the effort, how could it not?" He began to speak slower and softer.

"I love you, but I thought you were lost and confused because you never did. You did not know what you wanted and so you would not have any structure. Your life was uncertain because you were too carefree to have a plan." He paused, hoping that it didn't seem like he was trying to attack her. "Life played out how I planned it to. I had perfect friends who always supported me in everything, even the dumb stuff, but they were the reason that I was confident in everything that I did and confident in who I was. Then that dream just threw everything off course, and I was no longer myself. Life was not the same, it was chaotic because nothing made sense … I became lost … and it feels horrid."

Samara got out of her sleeping sack. She lay down next to him to hug him. He felt soothed and for the first time protected by someone else. As she hugged him, he felt that it was ok to let go of the pressure of perfection.

They slept peacefully that night. It could have either been the cathartic conversation or the protective bubble that Catori had placed around them to keep any other elements at bay.

The next morning, Catori was up before sunrise and made something to eat from the remains of the food they carried. Viyan woke up as the sun began to rise.

"Good morning," Catori said. "I broke a branch for you to brush your teeth with."

"Umm, thanks?" he replied.

"Maybe you can wake Samara up when you're done as the food will be ready soon."

"I'm up, I'm up!"

"Well, that's our food done!" Viyan said as he took his last bite.

"But I am still hungry!" Samara replied concerned. She turned to look at Catori with sad eyes.

"It is ok, we will reach our destination today. It is not much farther," she assured Samara.

They packed up their belongings to resume the journey and carried on heading North, following Catori's lead. Just over an hour into the next leg of their journey, they noticed how the forest around them began to change as they ventured further. It was becoming greener and fuller, just like they had seen in the fire.

"See how the trees are changing. Can you notice how the thin trunks of the trees are getting thicker and how the trees are becoming closer together? They are also not as tall as the ones we've passed. This means that we are moving into a newer land and getting closer to where we need to go," Catori explained.

They rode on for an hour or so more, talking and learning more about each other's backgrounds. Catori told them of the places she visited in America when she left her home. Of all the exciting things she saw and how it felt as though she had been living on an entirely different planet. It was the same Earth but the worlds were so completely different. "I remember feeling excited and lost all at once. I felt that I did not belong to that world, but I wanted so deeply to be a part of it. As a little girl, to see all the colours and developments so different to my home, fascinated me." Her tone changed from excited to sad. "But I knew that I could not stay, that I had a purpose to fulfil. And even though I did not want to leave, I made peace knowing that I would one day return."

"I can relate to feeling lost in a world. But a world that I have grown up in my whole life. It was a weird feeling because I was not unhappy in it, I just always felt like I belonged to another place. So I get the whole being a part of two worlds thing." Samara smiled at Catori. "I guess that we already have something that connects us."

The conversation turned to a short silence.

"I am getting really hungry now," Samara moaned.

"If we were at a river, I would hunt for fish and have some delicious nigiri. Yum!" she drooled, imagining the taste. Her daydreaming was abruptly broken by a rustle among the leaves.

They saw some movement in the low-lying bushes in between the trees and spotted what looked like it could possibly be a wolf. But it hastily fled before they could make certain. They caught a glimpse of it again and Catori gave chase on horseback. Viyan and Samara followed Catori as she chased the animal into the forest where they were met by a pack of wolves. It was as if they were lured there. They made eye contact with the pack, and the wolves standing side by side slowly moved toward them, all the time maintaining eye contact. The wolves then began to space out and surround them. They were ambushed!

"They have us surrounded! We can't move!" Samara exclaimed.

"Don't panic! Treat this as a welcome," Catori calmly told the two.

"These creatures are really smart and scary at the same time," Samara noted. "Wait! What do you mean a welcome!?"

Catori heard a rumble in the bushes and from the corner of her eye caught a glimpse of a man getting dressed.

"What?! What do you mean??" Samara asked impatiently.

"I just realised that it was a full moon last night," Catori replied.

"There is a pack of wild wolves surrounding us and you are suddenly being very cryptic! What. Do. We. Do?" Viyan asked in a panic.

Just then, the man walked out from the bush, all dressed. He was tall, young and handsome. He had thick black hair, sharp, deep eyes, tanned skin and a muscular build.

"Call back your pack!" Catori commanded him. "I am a Guardian," she continued.

"We wondered when you would come," the young man said.

With a gestured nod of her head toward the young man, as if to indicate that she was talking about him, Catori introduced the stranger.

"Meet the infamous *El Chupacabra*," she said.

Chapter Six

The Infamous El Chupacabra

The young man whistled to the pack and they dispersed. He walked up to the three and warmly introduced himself, "I am Liam of the Tamaska clan. How long have you been travelling?"

"It feels like forever," Samara replied slowly, captivated by his amber eyes.

"You must be tired. I'll take you to our camp to rest," Liam said as he gestured for them to follow him.

He walked them through the woods to his home.

"Is this where we needed to come to?" Samara asked Catori as they walked.

"Yes, the Lycans are one of the Guardians. At one time all of us lived together but for our safety, we had to go our separate ways. We lost contact over the years but before separating we were told where they would be and where to find them when the time came. I also believe that my Chief has in some way maintained communication with his," Catori explained.

"It was not safe for us to remain connected because it would be easier to track the Guardians then," Liam added.

He must have had really good hearing because Samara and Catori were a distance behind him, and they were talking softly to each other.

"But we did not move too far away because we knew that they would need us and our fighting capabilities to defend the rest. We are the better, fitter, stronger unit of the Guardians anyway," he said, giving Catori the side-eye before continuing.

As Liam led them to his home, he told them about his clan. "Lycans do exist, and we've been around for centuries, but the stories about us are not true. We do not hunt and kill people. We are part of the protective Guardians and what you caught sight of was a full moon initiation. A few of the younger members are learning to control their powers. But we'll explain all of this to you later."

They came to a reservation. It was similar to Catori's home although these were not tipis but log houses. A modern-built society that had a very wholesome feel.

"This is my home," Liam said as he pointed to a residence. "Come in and make yourself comfortable."

He helped tie up the horses and then led them inside. They entered from the living area which had black leather couches, a coffee table in the centre and a large flat-screen TV resting on a wooden TV console. A simple looking log house from the outside but a comfortable, contemporary living space inside.

"Why don't you freshen up and then we can head into town to get you some new clothes and something to eat," he told them. "After lunch I'll take you to meet our Chief."

"Look, I was not expecting this type of luxury on the journey, but at the same time, I am not complaining. Lead me to the bathroom please," Samara requested of Liam. "Do you have a spare toothbrush?" she whispered to him. "Tree branch bristles don't have a great reach," she said as she swished her tongue over her teeth."

Liam prepared to show them around town. When they went out their horses were gone.

"Where are our horses?!" Catori demanded.

"It's ok," Liam assured. They were taken to the barn to be watered and fed."

Viyan and Samara looked around nervously, unsure if they should trust Liam, but at sight of the other cabins they felt a sense of comfort. The settlement reminded them of a log cabin retreat that they would visit on family vacations in the wilderness, and it brought about a certain familiarity. Catori nodded in acceptance, believing Liam's response.

The houses were hidden within an enclosure of trees. Liam walked them through the woods, passing the other houses.

"So, we didn't exactly stay nature-based," he explained as they walked.

"Sell-outs!" Catori interrupted, her mocking accompanied by an eye roll.

Liam smiled as he continued, "We figured that because we were not sure of exactly when the prophecy would come true, we would 'evolve' with the times," he winked while using air quotes. "We tried to stay close to nature by living in the woods and in cabins, and we still kept our rituals in practice." He stopped as they got to the enclosure border. They could hear a bustling on the other side of the trees, although they could not see anything.

"But we had to progress," he said as he led them through a tree barrier. As they cut through the last trees, a different view awaited them on the other side. It was as though they were crossing through a door that led them into a completely different room.

Before them stood a fully functional small town. The town comprised of a few blocks of clothing shops, grocers, eateries and even a cinema.

"You must be hungry. Let's get something to eat," Liam said as he walked them toward *Lobo's Diner*.

They were led to a table by a young hostess, who was surely bunking school. She handed them the menus, followed by a mischievous smile directed at Liam.

"They have really good burgers and shakes here," Liam advised as they read through the options. A waitress came to take their orders.

"Ya'll new around here?" she asked the group.

"Hey Lupe," Liam greeted the young lady. "Yeah, these are my um … visitors," he replied. "Guys, this is my friend, Guadalupe," Liam said as he introduced the waitress. "We grew up together," he said with a smile as he looked at her.

"Ok, I'll have my regular, cheeseburger with a strawberry shake," Liam ordered.

"I haven't even looked at my menu so I will go with what he's having. But make mine double-thick," Samara told the waitress.

"Yeah, same for me. But can I get some grilled mushrooms and grilled onions with mine? Oh, and no pickles," Viyan ordered.

"Do you have anything vegetarian?" Catori asked, overwhelmed by the menu.

"Well, we're known for our burgers, but we can make you a grilled cheese and tomato sandwich or an avo-salad sub?" Lupe responded.

"I'll have the grilled cheese?" Catori questioned, uncertain of the choice.

"Yup, it's one of my favourites, apart from mac and cheese of course," Samara assisted her.

"It's been such a long time that I can't remember what's what," Catori explained, referring to her last visit to the outside world.

"Coming right up… in about 20 minutes," Lupe said with a snap of her fingers.

Liam turned to the group as the waitress left. "You've just met another werewolf."

"Who?! Guadalupe?" Samara asked.

"Yes, we learnt of our transformation around the same time and we've been learning and training together since."

"Is she your girlfriend?" Samara asked shyly.

"No," Liam laughed uncomfortably. "Lupe's like my sister," he said as he watched her go off into the kitchen. "And Tala our hostess, who is actually Lupe's little sister, was at the initiation this morning."

"But she is so tiny!" Samara commented.

"Oh, don't let that fool you," Liam cautioned. "Tala is probably the most gifted Lycan I have seen."

They looked at the young girl in surprise.

"She's gonna change things," he said admirably.

"So, where were we?" Liam asked. "Ahhh yes, I was telling you about the town." He continued to explain as he looked out through the window onto the High Street. "To the outside world we seem to live in a normal town. People pass through all the time, but we locals all know each other, and we have managed to keep it that way. We try to keep life in the town simple so that outsiders would not want to move here. There is a more developed city about 12 miles out and many of our townspeople work there."

Liam briefed them about the tribe's history. "At the very beginning, when we were selected as Guardians, Lycans were given shape-shifting capabilities, but over time some of the people have stopped evolving into wolves. Perhaps it's the diluting of the bloodline or just evolution, we are not sure. What you walked into this morning was the end of a ritual process which we enacted last night at the full moon."

Lupe brought in the drinks and Liam paused to take a sip before he continued. "You generally find out if you have the gene between the ages of ten and sixteen. We start to train those that are beginning to turn so that they can learn how to control and develop their powers. But once we know that someone is a wolf, they must attend after-school defence training. This tradition has been going on for generations. But as time's progressed and our tribes' people aged, some decided not to turn anymore. You see, the more you practise, the easier it becomes to control the mutation, it is something you can learn to do. So, many learnt to stop turning altogether. Most have just assumed normal lives, and some have even moved out of town to other cities or countries. My parents also travel out of town for work. Thankfully they come back home though," he laughed.

"I'm sure they wish they could stay away longer," Catori said under her breath.

"Super hearing!" Liam exclaimed, reminding Catori as he pointed to his ears.

"But how has no one discovered this town or your tribe?" Viyan asked.

"Well, we have learnt to control the turning, and in school the kids learn about our history and our way of life to protect the town from the outside world. Our beast-like counterparts appear only when necessary. I am not saying there have not been some slip-ups in the past but as time continued, we have become more careful, and because we live normal lives it is less conspicuous." He paused as their food arrived.

"Or perhaps we have just been lucky!" he added as Lupe served the meals.

"I think the most important aspect is to have a strong community. We refer to ourselves as Lycan, whether we can transform or not. And this is the reason that we still maintain a sense of clanship," he said before biting into his burger.

"A unified tribe is most important to help maintain a sense of purpose," Catori shook her head in agreement but did not make eye contact with Liam. She instead looked down at her meal.

"Ahhh, smells so good," Samara said as she opened her burger to pick out all the trimmings.

"These are delicious!" Catori exclaimed as she gobbled down her fries. "It's been so long!" she sighed.

"Wait!" Samara shouted. "You haven't tried it with ketchup yet," she suggested as she poured some on Catori's plate.

Yum!" Catori sunk back into her seat when she tasted the combination.

They laughed at her innocence.

"It is the simplest of things really," Samara declared as she tucked into her food.

Samara, Viyan and Catori explained their backgrounds to Liam over lunch. The siblings described how they had discovered their mission and Catori shared a shortened version of the story that she had told the two the night before. When she finished telling her tale, she took the last sip of her shake.

"Well, that was satisfying," she said as she put her glass down.

"The strawberry shake or the story?" Samara questioned.

"Both actually!" Catori responded. "The shake was amazing, but it is also such a relief to tell my story to you, it makes me realise that it is true. It gives me a sense of reality in a way," she expressed. "I have been so busy preparing for this journey all these years that it is somewhat difficult to perceive that I am now actually on it. I have just always followed this path, without thinking otherwise."

"I get what you mean," Viyan confirmed, comforting her as he placed his hand on hers. He looked at her and smiled before realising what he had done. He immediately pulled back his hand. Liam let out a loud burp, grabbing the attention. "Ohh, pardon me," he apologized with a fist to the chest. "Compliments to the chef," he shouted to the kitchen. When Lupe looked across and smiled Liam gestured for the cheque. He tapped his fingernails against the diner table as he waited for Lupe to bring it over.

Liam suggested that they make their way over to see the Chief first so that he could explain what the next steps were and then they could shop for everything that they may need for the journey ahead.

"The Chief will be in his office, so we'll head over there," he said as he led them out.

They walked across two blocks to a little house-let; the kind you would find along the strip of diners and shops in a little town, usually used for office space. Liam knocked on the door and then opened it up. He walked into a small reception area decorated with a big potted plant, a three-seater yellow couch and a small coffee table with magazines resting on it. Sitting at her desk, which was situated outside a room, was a middle-aged lady.

"Afternoon Aunt Kimaya," Liam greeted the lady, followed by a kiss on her cheek.

"How you been darling?" she asked.

"Great thanks. Is the Chief in?"

She nodded with a smile and offered, "Go right in."

Liam opened the door and walked into the room.

"Afternoon Papa," he said as he greeted the man with a strong hug. "I have some visitors here for you." Liam stepped to the side of the Chief so that he could see the three standing in the doorway and they could see him. An older gentleman, in his mid to late sixties, dressed in a shirt and jeans sat behind a desk. "Everyone, meet my grandfather, the Chief."

"Well, it's about time. I have gone grey waiting for this day," the Chief joked as he stood up from behind his desk. "So good to finally meet you all," he declared enthusiastically as he walked up to greet them. The old man gave them each a hug and then stepped back. "I cannot believe that this day is finally here. I cannot believe that you are here!"

"Neither can we!" Samara exclaimed caught up in the Chief's excitement.

"Yes, this all is still so … unbelievable," Viyan added.

"They need the full history lesson Pops!"

"I am sure they do. Let us get some fresh air," the Chief suggested.

He picked up his hat from the table. "Have you all eaten?"

"We've just gotten out of Lobo's and came straight to see you," Liam replied.

"You should have told me, I would have asked you to grab me a cheesesteak. I've been craving one of those. Anyway, at least I know what I am having for dinner."

"I doubt Grandma or Doctor La Flesche will be happy with that."

"And how will they find out?" the Chief winked, answering Liam who just shook his head and smiled.

At the back of the office grew a well-manicured garden. One side housed a big oak tree and a little wooden bench which the Chief would sit beneath to meditate and practise his rituals. Opposite the tree was a space resembling a small sunken arena. At the centre of this area sat a fire pit and surrounding the pit, large stepping-stones. Encircling that was a grassy stair in the ground with wooden pallets to sit on. This reminded them of the fire area of the Shamanic people. The group sat along the step and the Chief delineated his and Liam's history.

"We Lycans are listed as part of the Guardians and were one of the first tribes on Earth. When we came to be, we were known as the *Shapeshifters* of the Guardians. At first, we did not speak a verbal language, instead we used telepathy to communicate. The Guardians, along with all the first beings on Earth, functioned very differently from how we do today. But we, like Man, have also evolved over time. As the years passed, Man has called us many names, but *Lycan* stuck. There was no negative connotation to the word, it just described who we were and so we eventually adopted the name as ours."

The Chief avouched the role of the Lycans. They were given the gift of transformation and were meant to be the *link between Man and Beast on Earth;* to help each form live in unity and prosper on the planet. A Guardian who was half-man and half-beast was to provide humans with the knowledge of what it was like to be an animal, and to remind them that they were not the only forms of intelligence on Earth. While the Lycans initial role was to bridge the divide and aid the communication between species, with time, as Man began to evolve they no longer felt the need for this relationship. Man thought that he was better than all the other creatures – superior to the beasts that they once lived harmoniously with, and so the Lycans were ostracized.

"Humans began to consider us a threat and thus stories of us being evil and vicious began to circulate so that we would be avoided. Eventually they tried to eliminate us by hunting us down." The Chief paused.

"This is the habit of Man, to destroy anything that they do not understand. It is sad what ego can ruin, it is so blind to the truth," he sighed and shook his head before continuing.

"We could no longer try to help humans while our tribe was dying, so we went into hiding for our protection. As time passed, the Lycans were forgotten to have ever existed. But we are a strong people and despite all against us, we still thrive and continue on the tasked path," he proclaimed triumphantly.

"If you are so strong, why is it that so many of your tribesmen have left?" Catori asked.

"Of course, as the World evolved, we could not stop our people from living their own lives. How you live this life is your own choice after all. We had to make some rules to follow though. If anyone wanted to leave to go into the outside world, they had to first get the blessings of their fellow tribesmen, for their protection and the protection of the clan."

Catori smiled and nodded as she thought about this logic.

"You mentioned that you can control your ability to transform?" Viyan asked Liam.

"Well, I can now. And that is why I am training the young ones to do the same. It requires a lot of practise and a strong will."

When the Lycans were ostracized, they gave up their shapeshifting abilities because they began to see it as dangerous - as a curse. For the safety of the tribe, the elders asked the tribesmen to stop using their abilities and to stop their transformation. However, at every full moon, they would automatically change.

The Chief confirmed, "The full moon represents the end of a cycle, the point of change before a new phase is to begin. Transforming is embedded in our tribes' DNA and triggered by this phase of the moon. It is like a switch, forcing transformation. That is why Liam's role is so important. He helps the young ones learn to gain control of this automatic change."

"That Moon is one persuasive lady," Liam commended, looking toward the sky as he shook his finger at it.

"The Moon," the Chief resumed, "… is bound to the Earth. She is Her sister and Her protector. Without the Moon, the Earth cannot function. Since the creation of the Earth, the Moon was formed as Her shadow. She has always been there and just like She holds the Earth, She has a hold on us creatures, who like Her, are here to protect the Earth."

"Wow! How beautiful! It is all so very poetic," Samara whispered.

"When we first arrived, Catori had used the word El Chupacabra?" Viyan asked the Chief.

"Ahh yes! The infamous legend," the Chief expressed with raised eyebrows.

"That myth dates back a few decades when villages began to notice their livestock being killed from having their blood sucked."

"So that was a real thing? I've heard stories, but did it actually happen?" Viyan interrupted.

"Well sort of," Liam replied.

The Chief elaborated, "When the negative energy emanating from the Earth began to increase, it gave access for negative Energies from outside of Earth to enter. These Energies would replicate Earth's animals and one such replication was that of the vampire bat. These creatures would then cause the mutation of other bats and as a result of this, a few began to grow much larger in size. While vampire bats would usually ingest small quantities of blood from animals, because they were now much larger, they needed more blood for survival. They would puncture the livestock at the artery and ingest their blood, draining the animals completely till lifeless bodies were all that remained. Like bats, these creatures were nocturnal and would sleep during the day and come out at night. Because of this pattern they were not seen by humans. Only the drained corpses were found after the attacks. Conclusions were drawn as to what could have happened and stories were made up about the bloodsucker."

Liam continued the story, "When our tribesmen learnt of the creatures, we knew that we needed to stop them because they would only mutate further. My dad also had the role of transformation leader when he was younger. One evening he and his trainees went to seek out these creatures. They found a few at a farm attacking the animals. During the fight, one of our men were seen by a few humans. As they were dragging the creatures away from the farm, the owners awoke and caught a glimpse of what was happening."

Liam's voice changed to a deep, haunting tone, as if he was narrating *The Twilight Zone*, "And thus, the legend of the *El Chupacabra* was born. Sightings described a creature which was a mixture between a Lycan and the mutated vampire bat." He began to run his fingers across his chin, stroking an imaginary beard, "A vampire and a werewolf if you will."

The Chief intervened, "As the stories made their way around, there were more sightings. Various accounts of the creature created various descriptions. But simply explained, the Chupacabra does not exist. Only we do," he clarified, pointing to Liam and himself.

"That does clear things up somewhat," Viyan said intrigued.

"We have heard of werewolves in stories and movies, I just never in a million years thought that it was true."

He was starting to feel more comfortable unconsciously surrendering to the idea of the journey.

"Did you ever worry about being revealed, especially with so many of your tribe leaving to live their own lives outside of the clan?" Catori questioned the Chief again to gauge the reasoning for allowing his people to live so freely. Listening to his diplomatic rationale, she saw a refreshing perspective. All this time she had judged the Lycans for assimilating into the mainstream world. She felt that they did not remain true to their purpose by doing so. For her, by them giving up their original lifestyle, it meant that they were abandoning the Earth. Perhaps having a taste of the outside world again, she was rather more envious of them than disapproving.

"We were constantly worried. But as elders of the tribe we agreed that it was not fair to the individuals to stop them from choosing their lives. We were unsure when this event would even take place. We knew about it, it was why we existed, but there was no exact date of when it would occur. For all I knew, perhaps it was not going to even happen in my lifetime." The Chief paused. "The World was evolving, what if the reason for our existence had passed. We decided not to stop our tribesmen from living out their lives, but we vowed as leaders to protect the tribe and as a tribe to protect the Earth. The leaders could not forsake our mission."

Catori appreciated the wise words of the Chief. She always believed that the elders' wisdom was sacred and trusted their views. Maybe it was time to be kinder to Liam. She told herself that she would try.

"I am sure that the Shamanic people have explained to you that many different tribes and creatures form the Guardians. Those chosen for this mission each hold a sacred weapon which hides a crystal. When all the crystals are brought together, they will unlock the only force that will be able to stop the great *Rahu.*

Each Guardian knows the location of the next one needed for the mission and will lead you there.

The Chief paused to look at Catori and then he turned his gaze to Liam.

"As Catori is journeying with you on behalf of the Shamanic people, we will send Liam to accompany you on behalf of our people. Liam will guide you to the location of the next Guardian and so the journey will continue. Once you have all come together, you will represent the union of all the Guardians." He looked at them with pride. There was some shuffling between them as the words of the Chief began to sink in. The Chief took Liam aside and they spoke in private for a few minutes while Viyan, Samara and Catori chatted among themselves.

It was difficult for Viyan and Samara to digest their new role as it was such a big responsibility. A few days ago they were working in a store, leading normal lives. Living in a regular neighbourhood, doing the same things day in, day out. How could they go from that to this? From being ordinary one day to becoming *Guardians of Earth* the next?

Samara thought about how her whole life she knew that she was meant for more, that there had always been something missing. *But this?* It seemed so far-fetched. She was the girl who could not get people to stay in her life, the girl that was pretty much invisible. How could that girl be a protector of the Earth? The freaking big Planet in the sky – the actual, physical Earth? How could plain, simple, ordinary her, be a *Guardian*? Surely there was a mistake!

Her ponderance was interrupted as the Chief and Liam came back.

"I suggest that you stay the night and plan for the journey rather than leaving immediately," the Chief advised. "Besides, it's been so long, what's one more night? Everyone has been waiting eons for this day. I will gather us all for dinner in the town hall."

They looked at each other in agreement. They needed a good rest anyway.

"Let's stay around town and get some things for our trip," Liam suggested excitedly.

Though they were uncertain as to what they would need for the journey, they visited a few stores to gather equipment and accessories. It's not like they had an itinerary or any instructions on *how to save the Earth*. Liam put everything on a cheque for the Chief and the shop assistants threw in a few extra things, which they gladly accepted, just in case.

Liam invited them back to his house to freshen up for the town dinner. When they arrived, they were met by his parents. Liam had let them know about the trio's arrival and tea and snacks were laid out for them when they got back home. They joined his parents at the table and chatted over tea. It felt so comfortable, like visiting with one of their aunts and uncles. *We just met but they feel like family. Even from different areas of the globe, it's crazy how much alike people can be,* Samara thought to herself as she watched them laugh over something Liam said.

His parents caught them up on some familial history. Liam was a direct decedent of one of the first tribal Guardians and Liam's mom was the Chief's daughter. As Liam would have to take over from the Chief one day, like Catori, he had been very much a part of the tribal learnings. He was involved in training the young transforming wolves and actively bringing zestful energy into the tribe again. While Liam's parents, same as Viyan and Samara's, always knew that he would be a key figure in the protection of the Earth, they were not ready to send their son off.

In the evening, they made their way together to the town hall for dinner. They walked in to find the town's people already gathered in the hall, waiting for them to arrive. The crowd cheered loudly as they entered.

"Guess this ups the level of sendoff that you got from the last village you visited?" Liam smirked at Catori as he said this to Viyan while walking into the hall. Catori raised her eyebrows at his playful arrogance. *Be nice,* she thought to herself as she adjusted her plaits. The hall was decorated with posters of tribute made by the children of the town. As the group walked in, they were immediately flooded with the townspeople coming up to greet them. They felt like celebrities. While caught in conversations with the townsfolk, they smelt the delicious hot food being brought to the tables.

"Man, they're good! Look at all of this delicious food! How did they prepare it so quicky?!" Samara exclaimed to Viyan.

"Yes we are! And, you're welcome," Liam shouted from across the room. *Mmmm, I wonder if they're able to morph more than just their bodies,* Samara wondered to herself. *I sure could do with a gift like that*, she thought as she imagined the nursery scene from Mary Poppins, but instead of *tidying up* she would be able to zap up delectable dishes.

As the food was being served, the Chief walked up onto the stage in the hall to address everyone. He began his speech by illuminating the momentousness of the gathering. He reminded them how the tribe had lost hope, uncertain that the gathering would even happen. As he spoke, the four were being ushered by the crowd to the front. The Chief continued, "This right here is so special, history is currently unfolding with every moment going forward. It is such an incredible time for our tribe. We have been preparing many, many years for this day. Naturally we lost faith, but because of our kinship we managed to regain it, moving along still holding on to some glimmer of hope that it was not just folklore or a false belief. And let me tell you, as a leader, it has not been easy to keep that hope alive." He paused to look at the four and smiled at them, "But here you are. And here we are."

He turned back to look at the crowd and the crowd cheered.

"That moment that we kept working toward is finally here. We have stayed together and this is why we can stand here with pride and joy. Our hope may have waned and our beliefs questioned, but because we supported each other as a family we held the torch for all the Guardians. You are henceforth officially, ***The Guardians of Earth***."

The crowd cheered joyously as they felt the energy of the Chief's words. He turned to the four and raised his glass of beer. "Tonight, we toast you. You are about to follow through with what we as a tribe have been brought to this Earth for. We send you off with our blessings and our prayers. May your journey be safe and most importantly, may it be triumphant."

Everyone toasted the four.

"*Mabuhay!*" they all shouted.

"Tonight, we feast! It is well overdue!" The Chief paused.

"We have only been waiting generations for this meal," he concluded.

The crowd laughed as they sat down to share the food.

"Cheers!" Liam shouted as he took a swig from a can of beer.

The Chief came speedily by to grab the can away.

"None of that tonight," he cautioned. "You need to get a good night's sleep."

After dinner, the Chief quietly snuck the four out of the hall while the town spent the rest of the evening celebrating.

The next morning, they were up at sunrise to prepare for their journey. As they packed their things into the car, Samara sleepily commented, "It is going to take me a long while to get used to this '5 a.m. club', I do not see any benefits." She yawned. She was not a morning person; she could sleep right through it. They said goodbye to Liam's parents and the Chief. The Jeep was all packed and the three got in, allowing Liam time with his family in private. The Chief walked back to his car and returned with his spear. "So that I can be with you in battle," he said, handing Liam the sacred family weapon.

In the car, Viyan turned to the back seat to speak to Catori, "No offence Cat, the horses are cool and all, but I am so glad that Liam's parents gave us a car for the rest of the journey. Take it from someone who has not ridden a horse before this journey, it's not the best."

Before leaving the town, they stopped at the diner and walked directly to the same booth as the day before.

Lupe ensured that she got the early shift so that she could be there to wish them well. She came over to serve them.

"We better fill you up for your journey. Order whatever you like, it's on the house!" she said with a smile.

Samara placed her order, making sure to get plenty of food for the journey ahead as well. Catori looked at her as if to ask, *'Are you sure you are going to eat all of that?'*

"A doggy bag is always a good idea," Samara responded, as if she knew what Catori was thinking.

"Yeah, but that much?" Viyan asked.

"Well, she offered!" Samara defended meekly.

"That's ok, just don't share with anyone when they get hangry," Liam supported her. "Well except for me. Share with me okay!"

Samara smiled shyly.

"Besides, who knows how long the journey will be and when …" Samara paused as a thought crossed her mind "… and if, we will eat again!" she continued softly, taken by the notion that she did not know when their next meal would be. In true Samara fashion, a little dramatic when it came to food, but her concern was valid. They were going blindly into this mission. Fair enough, they were trusting the journey as suggested, but those *trust the process* type of journeys were usually about self-discovery and exploration. This journey had a purpose, a *stop the destruction of the World kinda purpose.* Shouldn't they at least know where they had to go? Wouldn't that help to accomplish their task?

"Actually," Liam broke her cogitation. "I know how long it will be. Well, I have a rough idea."

He knew where they needed to drive toward but the exact location was something that they would need to figure out together. After the celebration dinner the previous night, the Chief guided them where they needed to journey to next by plotting out a course for them to follow. As they ate, Liam mapped out the course. "It's roughly a day's journey to the coast - to our next destination," he confirmed.

After breakfast, they filled gas in the car and got some snacks from the filling station. "The way we're shopping, you would think that we're going on a vacation," Samara said jumping into the car, hands stacked high with sweets and snacks.

"I'm pretty sure you don't see it. You're the only one," Viyan pointed out.

"Road-trip!" Liam shouted as he started the car.

They drove for a long while, enthusiastic at first but a day on the road was exhausting and after a while, they got tired of talking and listened to music instead. A couple hours into the trip, Liam swapped places with Viyan. Samara was still unlicensed so she could not be much help behind the wheel. They made their second stop for petrol and got out to get the blood flowing again. Liam stretched out his arms as he yawned widely. "It's about another two hours to the destination, but I am really tired. Let's get something to eat and camp in the car till the morning. How do you guys feel about that?" he asked.

They nodded wearily in agreement.

"It will be too dark to get out at the coast anyway. Let's look for somewhere to eat and rest," Viyan added.

"I'll drive from here," Liam said as he jumped back into the driver's seat.

They found a little diner further down the road where they ate, in mostly silence, before heading back to the parked car for some sleep. At sunrise they awoke, somewhat rested, and freshened up in the washroom.

"I would gladly take that tree branch and the river water over this," Samara moaned to Catori as she tried to dislodge with her one shoe the toilet paper that stuck onto her other shoe. "I don't even want to know why that stuck to my shoe," she gagged, keeping herself from throwing up. The boys were waiting outside the car with some hot coffee and breakfast buns.

"Gimme!" Samara extended her arms like a Zombie as she walked toward the coffee.

They resumed the drive making their way to the coast. It was only another two-hour drive, but they were not as energetic as the morning before. Even Samara had nothing to comment about. They each just kept to themselves until they reached the coast. As they caught sight of the water, a feeling of familiarity suddenly hit Liam. He pulled onto a sand patch at the side of the road. The area was mountainous, and water could be seen below in the distance.

"Everything all right?" Catori asked concerned.

"I feel like I know this place, almost like I've been here before, but I am not sure," he responded, trying to recall if that was the destination.

He remembered heading out to that coastal place with his dad and grandad when he was just a little kid. It was a vague memory.

"I just need to get my bearings," he said as he drove again.

As they moved further down the road, they neared an opening among the trees bordering the water. Liam drove through the trees and then stopped a little way in.

"We should walk the rest of the way to the water," he suggested as he stopped the car.

They were not yet at the beach and had to make their way through some more foliage before they were able to get to the water. As they walked through the trees, the site was pristine and perfect with crystal blue waters.

"It is so beautiful," Catori said.

"It is!" Viyan confirmed.

They all stared, absorbed by the view.

"But it does not feel like the spot that we need to be at," Viyan said as he felt something pulling him away. "We need to drive a little more."

They made their way back to the car and further down the road. Liam drove and Viyan directed.

"The feeling is getting stronger," he noted, as they drove across the road parallel to the coastline. A few short minutes later he asked Liam to stop.

"I feel a pull toward that direction," Viyan said as he pointed to the spot. "We need to get down there."

They had stopped at a barrier at the side of the road. It barricaded a small opening to a little rocky cliff.

"You all get off. I'll look for somewhere to leave the car and meet you at the water," Liam told them.

As they got out of the car and walked to the metal barrier, they could see clearly how steep the walk down was.

"Yup, down there," Viyan said as he peered below.

The way down was filled with green leafy trees over a rocky base and while it was slightly steep, they managed to get down. They eventually reached the bottom and although they could see the water and smell the fresh ocean, a few trees blocked the direct view. Viyan led them to where he was being drawn toward. They walked a short distance through some sparsely growing trees and came out at a cove.

"Oh my gosh! This is gorgeous!" Samara exclaimed slowly.

Before them, a small cove led onto a lagoon and then opened into the wider ocean. The light shone over the cove and the hit waters, reflecting a glorious blue.

"This is it!" Viyan said knowingly.

Chapter Seven

Atlantis and the Atlanteans

They stared into the distance, admiring the splendor of the scenery.

Not another soul in sight.

"Sooooo, where exactly are we?" Samara eventually asked.

"I am not sure!" Viyan said. "I can just sense that this is where we need to be, but I don't know why."

"I do!" Liam called out as he made his way toward them.

"Do you believe in *mermaids*?" he asked the group.

"At this point, I believe in mermaids, fairies, pixies, even goblins and leprechauns," Viyan replied.

"It's funny you should mention those …" Catori said before quickly being interrupted by Liam.

"An adventure for another day, but today, we meet some mermaids."

As they followed him across the soft, white sand toward the shore, Liam began to explain how *The Atlanteans*, linked to the Mer-people, were part of the Guardians. They were the water-based Guardians as that was their territory to protect. They guarded the Sea-world against any threats. As Liam spoke, Samara noticed a few people swimming in the distance.

She did not pay much attention at first but then she observed how fast they were moving toward the shore. As they got closer, she could make out from their long hair and silhouettes that they were female.

"Errrh, guys!" she said nervously as she pointed to them.

One of the swimmers approached and leaned her torso onto a rock near to them, at the cove. The woman could have been a diver because she appeared to have on what looked like a type of wetsuit. She was gorgeous. Long flowing bright red wavy locks of hair and glistening skin, with very striking features. The four simply stared at her, uncertain of what to do or to say.

"We have been expecting you," the lady in the water said with a smile.

As she spoke her teeth were very prominent. She had noticeably tiny, pointed, sharp-edged teeth. Distracted by the lady's beauty, they were not aware that another three had approached the rocks as well. The three ladies remained submerged in the water so that only their heads and shoulders were visible. They all had glorious heads of hair, each with a distinctive shade; auburn, blonde and mousy brunette, but they all had the same bluish-grey eye colour. Their eyes had a misty glare as if there was a clear layer over them. Their beauty was hypnotic.

Suddenly, there was a startling noise from the water and as the three ladies surveyed their surroundings, their facial features began to change. They resembled wild cats about to attack. Their cheeks retracted slightly, revealing their sharp teeth and their eyes became more almond-shaped and darker in colour. They looked frighteningly aggressive. "It is nothing, just some big fish swimming to shore," the one with the red hair assured them, and at her words they calmed down.

"Are you the ones that we are here to meet?" Samara asked.

The one with the red hair replied, "Yes. We are here to receive you Guardians and take you back with us to our home. *To Atlantis.*"

The Guardians were concerned. While the ladies in the water had to be there to meet them - why else would they appear at the exact time and how did they know that they were Guardians - after seeing them in attack mode, they were not comfortable joining them in the water.

"I understand that you do not feel safe to venture with us, and you should be doubtful as this is all new, but I assure you, we are only here to guide you. My name is Eimear and I am army leader. Let me explain who we are to set you at ease."

The redhead elucidated that they were there to transport the four underwater to Atlantis where they would meet the ruler. "I am the leader of the *Sirens*, and they are part of my army," Eimear introduced, as she pointed to the women in the water.

She confirmed that it was because of Viyan that they were aware that the Guardians had arrived. Viyan was surprised, "*Me?*"

He tried to figure out how he could have let them know. He really couldn't have because he himself was not even aware till that the day before that their destination was the ocean. Surely these Sirens were mistaken. Sensing the confusion, Eimear clarified that everything would be revealed once they reached Atlantis. She looked directly into Viyan's eyes and a sudden sense of familiarity passed through him. He felt as if he knew her, and that she could be trusted. Eimear had a very diplomatic and calming nature about her.

"How will we go with you?" Viyan asked.

"We will take you there. You will swim with us," she replied.

Trying to assess the logistics of it, looking as though she were doing math equations in her head, Samara queried, "How would we be able to breathe under the water though?"

"You will breathe through your skin," Eimear confirmed.

Samara visualized her skin trying to breathe as a pair of lungs would - expanding and contracting. As she examined the skin on her arm more closely, Eimear continued, "We have with us the sacred conch of Atlantis and this allows non-Atlanteans, such as yourselves, to visit underwater." Eimear revealed a perfectly formed, pearl-shaded shell.

"Of course. Yes." Samara moved her hand back down, nodding as if she knew that that was what Eimear meant.

"Are you saying that we have to remain under for a while?" Viyan asked anxiously. "Like … I don't think … like … I can't … I don't…" he began to panic breathing heavily. "You don't understand, I *hate* the sea … I am afraid of it," he continued, somewhat embarrassed.

"You will be fine!" Eimear assured him and she looked directly into his eyes again. He instantly felt a wave of calm sweep over him.

Eimear instructed them what they needed to do. The group would need to get into the water with her and then extract air from the conch.

"Liam, this should be familiar to you," she said. "You have done this before."

Liam looked around, confused. He pointed to himself as if to ask, *Me?*

"You visited us with your dad and the Chief when you were younger, and we took you to Atlantis this very same way. But you may not remember much as you were still too young to understand."

Liam knew that he had been to the coast with his grandfather and vaguely recalled meeting a mermaid when he was younger, but he had no recollection of visiting Atlantis. Still, he trusted Eimear, it had to have been true. He would be the first to attempt the process.

Liam walked into the water to receive the conch from Eimear. He waded further till the water was chest high to meet her.

"Once you take a breath from the conch, you need to submerge yourself fully into the water. Because there is less oxygen in the water than in the air, you will need to consume oxygen through a larger surface area to distribute it more evenly and efficiently. You will do this using the pores on your skin and the process will get more oxygen into your body much faster."

The other three joined Liam in water before Eimear handed him the conch. He placed his lips on the opening, inhaling a deep breath through his mouth. Immediately he felt his nasal passages seal and a thin wall form at the back of his throat. His skin was coated with an oily, slime-like covering and beneath the substance, the pores on his skin enlarged slightly.

Liam began to vigorously tap his chest to let Eimear know that he could not breathe. Samara lunged forward to try to help him, but Eimear grabbed his arm so that he focused on her instead. Looking directly into his eyes, Liam calmed down before being submerged into the water. Eimear talked the others through the rest of the procedure. "Your lungs shall no longer be used while in the water. Therefore, your nasal passages and the back of your throat will be sealed so that water does not enter into your lungs. It may feel a little strange at first but do not think about what is happening, just surrender to the changes. The oxygen will move directly from your pores into your bloodstream, and you will have way more adrenalin and stamina. The deeper you go, the more pressure you will feel. As a result, you will take in less oxygen at first. But soon your body will adapt."

At this point, Liam was completely underwater while the others were still above. "Once you go beneath, a thin membrane will form over your eyes to help you see underwater. And the deeper you go, you will notice that your skin will take on an oilier, scalier, shinier appearance. This will help you manage the cold."

Liam began to panic again as the changes continued. Eimear went under water with him and held his hand to calm him down. As she looked into his eyes, he heard the words *calm, do not overthink, just surrender.* He relaxed and accepted the transformation, reminding himself, *You morph into a wolf, how difficult can it be to become a fish!*

Viyan, Samara and Catori each took a turn to use the conch, transforming the same way that Liam had. Eimear helped them into the water to adjust and once submerged, they could see the Sirens in full form. The Sirens were very much human on the upper half but from the waist down, their legs fused to form a tail. Because the suit covered their entire bodies - from neck to tail - they did not have a scaly lower anatomy as one would imagine a mermaid to have. The four Guardians did not have the same structure. Their transformations stopped at creating redundant lungs and slug-like skin.

Now altogether in the water, Eimear held her conch to her lips and blew in their direction. The surrounding water became choppy before it parted, forming an air bubble around them. Contained in the bubble, their clothes fell away leaving them in a type of swimwear just before their bodies were suited. A material slowly worked its way from their toes to their necks. It was a skintight suit that resembled the material used for scuba diving apparel, though it was much lighter. Lightweight and comfortable yet at the same time insulated and armoured. The four were now wearing the same suits as the Sirens.

As they were led through the lagoon and into the sea, each of them was prompted to grab hold of a Siren's shoulder. When they did, they were swept down into the water at magnificent speed. They swam deeper and further into the ocean until they reached the middle of the Atlantic. The four Guardians felt a tingling on their bodies as they delved to deeper depths. They noticed their skin getting scalier as a covering began to form over it, protecting it from the icy cold waters. The deeper they swam, the darker the water became. They slowed down and Eimear used the conch to create a pathway. She blew into the shell and it created a small porthole in the water for them to swim through. She had opened a doorway to her home, lessening their journey time there. As they neared the ocean floor the consistency was murky, but they were still able to see the bright lights emanating from down below. The moment that they saw it in the distance, the Guardians instinctively knew that it was Atlantis.

The Sirens slowed down their pace as they led the Guardians to an underwater city. At the realisation that an entirely separate world existed beneath the water, swimming closer, they became aware that that civilisation had lived and thrived for eons below. More so, they realised that humans were oblivious to its existence. In this state of awareness, the same thought crossed all of their minds at the same time. *Earth is made up of over 70 percent water. Because humans have been unable to explore all of the Earth's waters, there is so much of the ocean that they do not know about. There is more that goes on below the sea than on land.*

The Guardians looked confusingly at each other before becoming aware that someone was communicating through their thoughts. *It was Eimear.* She explained that as they could not talk underwater, they used telepathy as a means of communication. Just like the other creatures of the sea, Atlanteans used sounds and gestures, but they had been given the gift of telepathic intuition as well.

As they swam further down toward the city, Eimear told them about how her army came to be. "You may have heard about us Sirens, but I can assure you that the stories are not altogether true. We live with the Atlanteans under the sea and it is our duty to protect them and the ocean. But we are also here to protect Atlantis from absolutely everyone. We used to do this mainly from underwater but then came a time when this approach would no longer suffice. As Man evolved they took to the seas, for food and discovery. Voyagers would often travel across the seas in search of new lands. If adventurers got too close to Atlantis, we would take subtle measures to keep them away."

Eimear explained how the Sirens used their beauty and power of singing to hypnotise and distract adventurers. They would never harm anyone unless absolutely necessary. The Sirens were very alluring and would use this to their advantage to draw people away from their waters. But when the legend of Atlantis spread, explorers began to seek the lost city. They learnt of the mysterious land and stories of fortunes that it housed. Many came close to discovering Atlantis and so the Sirens merely lured these people away from the ocean deep. Sadly, this was not the version that got retold. Because the Sirens were unfamiliar creatures, sailors and their like would try to capture them. In retaliation, the Sirens would assume their beast-like features. They had razor teeth and sharp coral claws that would form in defence, and they would use this to attack any captors. Because of these occurrences, the tales retold depicted the Sirens as evil and vicious. The one thing that these stories did though, was keep the explorers away.

Initially, Sirens used to have wings and were able to fly above and sound a warning if danger was approaching. But as time went on, they remained more and more in the water and eventually these wings disappeared. As they lost this capability, they began to rely more on their fighting skill and became instinctively more defensive. They no longer used song as a weapon but physical fighting became their method. They had evolved into a militant army. But Eimear was wise and gentle and wanted the Sirens to learn balance again; to go back to their natural ways. She taught the Sirens that not every creature of difference was a threat.

"Our world has changed significantly as the years have passed, the same as yours has, but our mission has remained the central focus of our existence. We protect the waters and now part of our mission is to protect you too. Let us take you to our home and you will see it for yourself."

As they approached, Atlantis became visually pronounced, glittering below the murky sheath. The water surrounding the city was clear, as though it was in a bubble of its own, separated from the surrounding seawater. The city was beautiful, architectural and bright. It was far more detailed than what they imagined it would be. As they swam through the city absorbing its exotic sights, they were in disbelief that they were there– deep below on Earth's Ocean floor. It was hard to grasp that it was Earth, it felt more like they had been transported to a mystical realm. The buildings were huge structures made from white marble. Edifices, some of which were in ruins, resembled structures from ancient Greece and Rome and stood central to the city. On the outskirts, smaller structures carved out of stone and coral stood. These looked as though they could be the homes of the Atlanteans.

The Sirens swam toward the middle of the city where an ancient-looking temple structure stood. It was well guarded by beautiful Sirens who gave them way when they saw Eimear. The group were led inside and greeted by the splendour of the gold and rich blue and green colour accents. They noticed how their suits complimented their surroundings, golden-hued like the colour of Atlantis. The group were escorted to a cavernous room, the ceiling held up by marble pillars. Further within the room sat a magnificent coral and limestone carved throne. And on the throne sat a king, an actual king - one who donned a crown and held a lustrous triton in his hand. They were awestruck.

"Wow, just like *King Triton* from The Little Mermaid," Samara whispered in her mind.

The King was waiting for them to arrive and stood up from his throne to greet them as they entered the room. He was very much how they had imagined he would look; middle-aged with a greying beard, and he was mighty.

The King welcomed them, "I am King Nereus, the current ruler of Atlantis."

They heard the King's voice in their heads, but it was as though he was speaking out aloud and it echoed as it would have in the enormous, empty room. Liam automatically bowed at his deep, heavy voice.

"Let us retire to the common room, we use this old room and throne to make a good first impression. It's just for the effect." The King sounded a deep roar of laughter.

"Well it definitely worked, you've made an effective first impression," Liam responded nervously. The King looked at him directly. He was taken aback, unsure of how he was able to respond, not with words but in thought. *And how did the King hear him if he thought it?*

King Nereus stood up and towered over them. He had a demanding stature. But it was not that which grabbed their attention. The King was dressed in the same clothing as they were, his was just pure gold in colour. It fit snuggly over his body, emphasizing his muscles and his *separated* legs. He looked completely human - just like them.

They were led into a room and to a colossal table made from limestone. The whole of Atlantis was probably fed at this table, it was that big. In fact, everything was on the rather larger scale in Atlantis. They sat down on the matching limestone calved chairs covered in sea sponges for cushioning.

"This is super comfortable - so soakable. No wonder *Spongebob SquarePants* is always so happy," Samara thought. She heard laughter in response.

"This is so strange! It is like we are having conversations without using any words. And we can all *hear* each other, at the same time," Viyan responded.

"It is one of our methods of communication and because you have temporarily assumed our DNA, we can use this means to communicate with you. It is strange at first, but you do get used to it," the King explained.

"But how is it that we can't hear all of the thoughts running through our minds?" Catori asked, trying to make sense of their *magic*.

"For instance, how hungry I am," Samara added.

"The words that you would have spoken out loud, those are the only thoughts that get shared," the King confirmed.

"It makes no difference in Catori's case, cos she has no filter," Liam mocked as he acted out laughter, and while no sound physically came out, they could hear him laugh.

"How advanced!" Samara noted.

"It is in fact very ancient. This method of communication was used by some of the very first people of Earth," King Nereus exclaimed matter-of-factly.

He proceeded to give them a summary of Atlantis and explained its history and the Atlanteans' involvement as Guardians. He described how the triton was one of the instrumental elements in the protection of Earth and that was why they had to ensure its security.

"Atlantis once existed as a continent above the water. We existed long before ancient Greece and Rome but when our lands dissipated into the sea, our history lived on through their heritage and in their infrastructure and culture. You will see this still today. Because some of our people stayed above water to create those lands, they carried our legacy. It lived on through their stories and in their practises. Our history lives on through theirs." While the King communicated all this information telepathically, his facial expressions articulated what he was relaying.

"Our time on land was shared with some other races before the advancement of the human race. We lived in harmony with so many of these races on Atlantis but when the threat had fallen upon Earth, the Guardians were given a task to protect the humans so that they would not evolve to bring forth the destruction of the Earth. We Atlanteans were asked to protect the seas. That is when Atlantis sank ocean-deep. Some who did not want to take on the tasked responsibility moved on to other continents to guide humans in developing new lands. The rest of us ascended to the depths of the seas. When Atlantis was above water, we lived in peace with other races like the Mer-people who lived in our surrounding seas. Now we live together with them below the water, and we all protect the seas as one."

As Eimear had revealed, the ocean is vast and has largely uninhabited territory. Taking advantage of the open space, portals would open allowing other planetary creatures to enter. It was because of this that the Atlanteans and Mer-people, with the defence of the Sirens, were in constant guard of the sea, trying to protect the planet against the negative Energies slowly taking over. The advantage of the ocean was that because not many of the other planets had such large bodies of water, creatures were unfamiliar with it and so very few could enter and survive in the water. The negative forces trying to come to Earth would do so mainly via land.

The King turned to look directly at Viyan and then moved closer to him.

"You are not aware, are you?" he asked, communicating with Viyan only.

Viyan had no idea what the King was asking and shook his head to indicate *No.*

"You were once a *Prince of Atlantis*," the King told him.

Viyan just looked at King Nereus and nodded. First the Sirens and now the King - they definitely had him confused with someone else. *Him, a Prince! An underwater Prince?* It was laughable. Heck, they were lucky enough that they managed to get him into the water. No way he had ever lived in it. The King stood back, explaining to them all that Viyan was a prince in a previous life and that Atlantis was once his home. He turned back to Viyan. "Your second name, *Varunesh* means *Lord of Water.* You would have made a strong leader here but when you saw how humans were changing, you chose to leave Atlantis so that you could join the mission on land to protect the Earth."

Since the beginning of modern Earth, mermaids and mermen have existed. When the Atlanteans moved to the water, the Mer-people helped them learn about life in the ocean. They lived as one, protecting the seas as their joint mission. Like the other Guardians, they were brought to Earth to guard it and just like the others they knew that a time would come when Earth would need saving. Viyan was once an Atlantean but chose to live as a human to fight and protect the Earth when that time would come. The reason that Viyan feared the sea was so that he would stay away from it. He developed an irrational fear preventing him from entering its waters, for if he did, he may have felt at home and never returned to land and to his mission. His purpose would then be forgotten.

Viyan contemplated the information. It was true, he did feel different in the water, a feeling he could not explain, but in no way was it the reason the King had given. *He, was an Atlantean? A Lord of the water?* No!

Eimear joined them in the room and handed the sacred conch back to King Nereus. He signalled one of the guards. Moments later a beautiful young mermaid with locks of glowing red hair and shimmering tail swam in. They all were struck with her beauty and watched as she swam toward the King. He asked her to place the conch back where it belonged and then called the others to introduce her to them.

"This is my daughter, Nereida, the youngest of my children."

She smiled and bowed her head before taking the conch from her father. They watched on as she shimmered away. She looked magical. Samara wondered aloud how the Atlantean King, physically human, had a mermaid daughter.

"Perhaps his wife was a mermaid," Liam replied to Samara.

But the King did not respond to their curiosity.

As he tried to process what he had learnt about himself, Viyan went over to the King.

"Why can't I remember anything?" he asked." Anything about this life nor about the ocean? Nothing you have said is familiar. I think you are mistaken."

"Come with me. Let me show you something," the King comforted.

He led Viyan as they swam out through the building and into the city. Eimear followed to protect them but gestured for the others to stay behind.

They swam over the buildings and the King took Viyan to a slightly secluded space, close to the edge of the city. A rocky patch with a few boulders covered with bright coral and seaweed. King Nereus stood atop the highest boulder and Viyan followed. He gestured for Viyan to stand across from him. He then handed over the triton. Viyan hesitated but took it. The moment his hand touched it, a wave-like force blasted out. The two were encapsulated in a glow of light and Viyan began to download information about his past life through the power of the triton.

The visions entered his mind, taking him on a journey of discovery. He saw the life that he had lived in Atlantis, many, many years ago. Visions of Atlanteans that he knew caused a warmth of familiarity to brush over him. He could feel how happy he was in his life under the water. In his vision, he was guided to a house. His house. He swam into his old room and touched items from the life he used to have. From the corner of his eye, he saw movement in the room. When he turned toward it, he caught his Atlantean reflection in the mirror. He floated in front of the mirror, just staring at his reflection. After some time, the light faded and Viyan came to. He looked at King Nereus and then lunged forward to hug him. "I remember everything!"

The two swam back to the palace where the others waited. Viyan took Samara aside to explain to her what had happened.

He was so hyped, excited by what he had witnessed. It was crazy and wonderful all at once. Firstly, that he existed in another lifetime and secondly, that he had lived a life underwater - the one place that he feared. Once the euphoria passed, he felt confused and uncertain if it was true. The doubt flashed over his mind, making him question the reality of everything; that he once was another person, living a whole other life with a different family. *If he had another family, what had happened to them? Where are they now? Are they still in Atlantis? Could he meet them?*

Catori and Liam came over when they saw Viyan getting agitated.

"Are you ok?" Catori asked concerned.

"Yeah, what happened with the King? You ok?" Liam questioned.

Viyan explained what the King showed him and then expressed his difficulty in trying to make sense of it all.

"I suppose it is overwhelming to learn your past and have such a short time to process the information. With Liam and I it is different because we have always known this life and the possibilities that come with it. I guess nothing is too strange for us."

"Cat is right. It is different for us. But let me give you some advice. Don't try to make sense of it because you never will. You either accept it or you don't, but there is no in-between. The in-between is where the confusion lives."

"Wow, Liam! That is some good advice," Samara complimented.

"Well, I am the expert of in-between; *half-wolf-half-man*," Liam winked at her.

Viyan felt better. He thanked them for helping him work through the myriad of emotions and questions that came with the new information. It was good to have a support system again!

"I guess it's back on the journey," he said with a deep exhale.

They approached the King to guide them to the next destination. All that they had learnt so far was that the Mer-people were part of the Guardians and that this once included Viyan. But they did not know what information the merfolk kept that would aid them on the next leg of their mission. The King called his daughter back into the room. Again, they could not help staring as she swam in. King Nereus spoke, "Nereida was born 17 years ago. A prophecy among our people was that a mermaid with transformational abilities would be born to an Atlantean family. Abilities that would link the land and sea. We Atlanteans are genetically human, historically from the land. The Mer-people belong to the water. Nereida is both; she is of the sea and can assume full human functioning above the water." He recalled her birth. "Nereida was born a human baby; born with legs. Her tail only formed months later, and it was then that we knew she was the prophecy come true. She was part human, part mermaid and the one who our legend predicted would bridge the land-sea divide. You see, mermaids live in the water, and they cannot transform into humans. But Nereida can." He paused to turn to his daughter. "She is special," he said as he held onto her shoulders. "We knew that the birth of the *chosen one* would signal the time that the Guardians would need to come together. Thus, when Nereida was born, we understood that the prediction was coming true and that soon the Guardians would be uniting."

The King turned to look at Liam. "This was the time that you remember coming to Atlantis with your father and grandfather. You came to visit Nereida and for us to start preparing for this exact time."

Liam could now vividly remember that visit to Atlantis.

King Nereus looked back at them all. "She will join you on your journey and represent the Atlanteans and Mer-people in the fight for Earth."

Liam looked at Nereida and smiled, "Don't worry, I know what it's like to bridge a divide."

Nereida joined them as they left Atlantis. But before they could leave, King Nereus held Viyan back.

"You are going to need this!" he exclaimed, handing Viyan the triton.

"I cannot take this, it belongs to you, it belongs to the sea," Viyan hesitated.

"It does. But it also belongs to you!"

Viyan looked at the magnificent weapon in his hand, feeling its power.

"You can return it, once your mission is done!"

The King explained that Nereida would lead them to their next Guardian. He kissed and hugged her and bid them all good luck.

"We're a full team now, like a mini gang," Samara shrieked excitedly, as they swam off.

"Maybe our gang needs a cool name," Liam replied.

"Like *The Fab Five*? Or *Fantastic Five*?" suggested Samara.

"I think that one's taken?" Liam corrected her.

"Maybe *The Defenders*?" Viyan asked. "That is what we are, isn't it? We have to defend The Earth."

"I like it!" Catori agreed as she smiled at him.

Nereida confirmed that they would not be heading back to the shore as they needed to swim through the ocean to the next destination.

"But we left all of our belongings in the car!" Viyan exclaimed.

"Yeah, especially our food!" Samara cried.

"It is ok, you have your most necessary belongings with you," Nereida comforted.

She turned to each of them and pointed to their weapons as she accounted for them, "Liam, you have your spear and Catori has her bow and arrow. Now Viyan has his triton and I, my conch. This is all we need."

"I did not realise that everyone has a weapon. Where is mine then?" Samara humbly asked.

"I am sure that you will get your weapon soon enough, but we need to get moving if you are to." Nereida gestured for them to swim faster.

Samara was stoked. She wondered what it could be. *A sword? A shield like a superhero? A cool blade knife, or … nun chucks!?* She could not wait to get to the next destination.

Accompanied by the Sirens, they followed Nereida as she swam into the ocean. Each Defender grabbed a hold of a Siren's shoulder, preparing to be whisked away. The speed started off slow, allowing them to capture the beauty of the ocean deep. An array of coloured coral decorated the ocean floor, and beautifully shaded fish swam in their little schools. Fish species which they had never seen before reminded them how little of the ocean they knew. Various shapes and sizes; bright colours, translucent, shimmering metallic colours and even colour-changing chameleon fish, all swimming below in a world of their own. They could never have imagined that it was this vivid. It was entirely different to the ocean that humans knew. It was luminous, animated and intelligent.

As they admired the views, a school of dolphins playfully raced beside them and then joined them to journey together the rest of the way. The dolphins and the Sirens seemed to be communicating telepathically because a few began to chatter and then swam off. A few minutes later they joined with a narwhal.

"Narwhals are really good navigators, they have the best echolocation of the ocean and can guide us where we need to go," Nereida explained when the whale joined them. "Narwhals are our unicorns of the sea. You will notice that a lot of land creatures are replicated in the sea. For example, eels are our snakes, mermaids replicate humans while narwhales replicate unicorns and even have some of their characteristics, like a super strong sense of awareness. That's why the narwhal is the best at navigation," Nereida explained.

I don't think she knows that unicorns are just a myth, Samara thought to herself as she looked over at the narwhale, wondering if there was some truth to what Nereida was suggesting.

The Sirens picked up the pace as the whale guided them across the ocean. It was a rather fast swimmer for something the size of mini-van. The distance back out was further than the swim to Atlantis, and because they were not travelling at *Siren-speed* for the benefit of the narwhal and dolphins accompanying them, the voyage was taking much longer. But, they had managed to travel through the Strait of Gibraltar toward the Atlantic Ocean once more. They had left Atlantis through the Mediterranean Sea and were crossing back over into the Atlantic.

Unexpectedly, the dolphins and the narwhal began to sense something.

"What's wrong?" Nereida asked, as the whale motioned its head.

The water began to darken. Hesitant and nervous, the animals pre-empted that something was about to happen. The dolphins communicated their concern to the Sirens who cautioned everyone to slow down. Suddenly, the water began to churn and a whirlpool formed nearby. At sight of this, the Sirens instantly knew what was happening.

"It's a portal!" Eimear shouted, warning the others.

The portal forced open and in a sudden rush, creatures swam out as if they were being hurled into the ocean. The Sirens assumed their military mode but were outnumbered by the beings making their way into the water. They were alien. Reptilian-humanoid looking beasts, armed with weapons. Their bodies were human in structure but they had webbed appendages. Their skin, thick and greenish blue, resembled that of an alligator, and similarly, they had tails and lizard-like facial features.

The moment the aliens spotted the Defenders and saw the Sirens with their spears, they attacked. They drew their weapons and fired off laser beams at the group. Instinctively, the Sirens formed a protective line in front of the Defenders. Eimear stood dead centre in front of them, assuming a shielding stance. With her arms beside her as if she was pushing against the water, she tightened the muscles in her body to build up resistance. Doing this, she generated an energy within her which she released through a powerful scream. The scream, muffled by the water, was intense enough to cause rippling sound waves. The waves acted as a protection field, shielding them from the lasers. The aliens moved forward to attack and the Sirens drew their spears to fight back. But there were only six of them and they were outnumbered almost eight to one. They tried their best but there was no way that they could fight off these creatures.

Narwhals usually travel in pods and the rest were close behind the Defenders when the attack happened. When they reached the battle scene, they joined the dolphins to assist in the fight. The dolphins used their noses and heads to slam the aliens in their torsos while the narwhals used their tusks as a sword, slicing and stabbing the beasts. But they too were no match for the aliens. These creatures were strong, with powerful tails for extra weaponry. Liam and Catori tried to assist but the ocean was difficult territory for them to fight in. They were afraid and had no idea how they would even be able to fight underwater, but they tried regardless. Liam held on to a dolphin which dragged him through the water as he swung his sword against the enemy. Just as they were losing hope against defeating them, they heard a shrill, piercing cry and began to feel instability in their surroundings. In the distance, they saw a monstrous beast approaching. Viyan, Samara, Catori and Liam were certain that this leviathan would be the death of them. They noticed how the Sirens were drawing back from fighting as the monster neared. *Were the Sirens giving up hope too?*

The monster fast approached, waving its gigantic arms.

"It's the Kraken!" Nereida exclaimed with relief coupled with a sense of pride. The colossal creature tore through the aliens with ease, fighting them off with each swipe of its arms. The Sirens were the seas' army, but the Kraken was their weapon of defence. It scoured the oceans, protecting it from danger, but it always came to the Sirens' rescue. The Kraken was akin to a machine, able to fight off every attack. It camouflaged itself on the ocean floor and moved across the seas keeping a watchful eye. Like all the mythological creatures so far, the Kraken was not evil or a blood-thirsty monster, although it did look like one. It resembled a giant squid with an elongated head, which helped it swim faster in the ocean, but it also had the properties of an octopus. With its long and powerful, muscular yet flexible arms, it was able to grip, fling and crush. The suckers on its arms enabled it to climb objects, and venomous hooks allowed it to grip onto and kill any threat. It also had whip-like tentacles that it used for protection. Its giant eyes, each roughly in diameter the size of a dolphin, allowed it to see far and exceptionally clearly underwater. Like the octopus, it could cause a distraction by simply releasing ink into its surrounding area. It was a magnificently designed weapon, but make no mistake, it was a monster.

The Kraken easily fought off the aliens but just as they were almost all destroyed, two more portals opened, and they came pouring out in droves. The Kraken fought them off but with the realisation that they were not easing up, it created a distraction by clouding the area in black ink. Still able to see, it motioned one of its tentacles toward the Defenders, who were huddled up by the Sirens. The monster grabbed them and just like a catapult, flung them within the waters. Using one of her gifts, Nereida was able to manipulate the water. She created a protective energy field around them as they were being tossed. They were thrown with such force that they cut through the water at incredible speed. As their momentum eventually reduced, Nereida was able to bring them to a comfortable stop.

Gaining their bearings from the rollercoaster ride, Nereida checked to ensure that everyone was ok. She had felt a change in the water and knew that they had been moved across seas. Assessing their location, she learned that they were close to their destination. "We are at the edge of the Celtic Sea. It is not too far away from here," she confirmed. Though exhausted, they had no choice but to continue their journey. Making their way through the water, Catori detected some movement behind them. "We are being followed," she yelled.

A few alien creatures had become trapped in the after current that had carried them and were now in pursuit. The Defenders were uncertain what to do as the Sirens were not there to protect them. They were on their own. *How would they fight them off?*

The aliens were fast swimmers and drew quickly close. As they neared the Defenders, they aimed their weapons, ready to attack. In that instant, something came dashing through the water from behind the aliens, in full view of the Defenders. This creature was heading straight at them. A long, wide, snake-like being - it definitely was one of the reptilians and it was aiming for them. The Defenders turned around to swim away. There was no way they were going to make it, but they had to try. Just as the creature was about to crash into the Defenders, it swam around to the front of them instead. There it protectively wrapped itself around them. As it did, its gigantic tail pushed the aliens deeper into the ocean. It continued to coil its body around the five and swam them further into the ocean. The snake did not stop till it reached a smaller enclosure. No one had any idea what was happening because it was all happening so fast. *Were they even being rescued? They couldn't tell anymore.*

As the creature swam away with them, Nereida sensed a slight change in the water once again as they moved from the Celtic Sea into the Irish Sea. She was right, it was getting colder. The creature began to slow down and they were unsure of what was going to happen when it came to a complete stop. When it did stop, they were stunned at their rescuer's identity. As it gently pulled its tail away and moved its gigantic body in front of them, they could see it clearly. The creature was a mix between a giant snake and a seahorse – with a less pointed face. "This is Nessie!" Nereida presented, as she touched heads with the creature. "*The Loch Ness Monster*, the friendliest monster I know," she announced as she looked at the creature in adoration. "Nessie guards the lakes for us. She is not as lethal as the Kraken, but she is our dedicated protector of the lochs. And she has taken us exactly where we need to be. She rests mainly in these waters because it is from here that she protects these precise lands that we are going to. She guards against any threats that may come from the seas," Nereida explained as she lovingly stroked the creature's head.

Following Nereida's lead, they moved closer to the shoreline preparing to get out of the water and onto land. "Within these woods live the next Guardians," she said. The water became shallower as they moved to the banks. Nereida took out the conch that she wore around her waist in an enchanted sling-like pouch made from seaweed and coral. The conch was protected like a pearl in an oyster shell and seemed to open only with a touch from Nereida. She handed the conch to Liam who ingested air from it. As he did, the pores on his skin began to seal and he could no longer breathe beneath the water. His nostrils opened up and water began to enter. Liam jumped out of the lake and climbed onto land, where he lay, coughing up the water he had choked on. Next, Viyan used the conch and soon he too was his normal human self. Samara and Catori followed. The reversal process was much quicker than transforming into an Atlantean.

Samara leapt out of the water and onto land. "Oh my gosh, that is freezing!" she cried, feeling the icy water on her face.

"You spoke!" Liam exclaimed. "Like actual words came out of your mouth."

"This is like the best part about being human!" Samara acknowledged.

"Especially for you," Viyan laughed.

The moment that they transformed back to human, they experienced the cold water on their sensitive skin even more. Despite the sunny weather, the water was icy-cold. Like lizards, they lay in the sun absorbing the heat to regulate their body temperature. The suits dried almost instantly but the Defenders needed to acclimatise.

Nereida moved closer to the land in preparation for her transformation. She raised her upper body out of the water and this was followed by a noticeable shimmer within the water. Like Liam, she could control her transformation at will. Her metallic bronze tail was split into two legs and her suit now covered her legs, just like the others. And just like a human, her skin transformed from having somewhat visible pores to them being almost invisible. The film over her eyes disappeared revealing their piercing, aqua-blue colour. Before fully stepping out of the water, she turned around to give a thank you nod to Nessie, who although deeper in the water, was still watching them. Nereida stepped into the sun and her skin instantaneously changed from a pale, almost translucent tone, to a golden shade. As she had not been exposed to the direct sun for a long time, her skin protected itself by darkening its colour and her hair adjusted from a titian shade to crimson-red under the sun's rays. Everyone was in awe as she changed from mermaid to human because she was equally captivating in both forms.

As their body temperatures settled, they stood up from the ground. Catori almost tripped and Viyan instinctively caught her arm and helped her balance. "Thank you," she said with a smile.

"Yeah, these dang sea legs will do that to you," Samara expressed as she wiggled her feet.

Nereida walked up to them.

"Look atcha, look atcha! There's something different. I can't quite put my foot on it," Samara acted out to Nereida, quoting a scene from *The Little Mermaid*.

"She's got legs, you idiot!" Liam shouted, and then he winked at her.

Samara did not expect that he would have watched The Little Mermaid let alone remember it. Made sense though, it probably was something he could relate to as a kid. Samara imagined him glued to the T.V as a child, rewinding the scenes and constantly replaying them. *How cute little Liam was*, she thought.

They followed Nereida from the riverbank into the woods, which were a little further inland. "It is going to be tricky from here," she said. "This is the right place but there is no exact location of where the next Guardians are. I just knew to come here."

"Let us see if we can help," Catori said. "Liam and I grew up among nature, perhaps we can figure something out."

Catori and Liam walked in front of the others, discussing what they thought of the woodlands in front of them. The area was untouched, so it was difficult to determine a path to take. They both were not sensing anything either. They agreed to walk a little further to the heart of the woods to hopefully gain more insight to the direction they should go.

"You know I'm just following your lead right," Liam whispered to Catori. "I have no idea where I'm going. Sure, my woods I know. It's the only home I've had, so I know it like the back of my paw," he smiled. "But I'm actually not very good at tracking. It's my weakest … strength," he added not wanting to seem incapable. "You're better at the nature stuff!" he told her.

Catori smiled widely at him before nodding her head as if to say *thank you*.

"My mind is still boggled by how we were able to breathe underwater," Samara said. "I still can't get over the whole experience!" she continued, raising her hands to the sides of her head, gesturing her bewilderment.

"I still can't get over the fact that we went to Atlantis," Viyan responded.

"Well, I can't get over the fact that you ARE FROM ATLANTIS," Samara shouted.

"Oh! And what about you?" she said, as she turned to Nereida.

"What do you think of being on land? This is all so new to you. What does it feel like to talk? Can you still use telepathy? Oh! And it must feel so strange to have legs?" Samara listed the questions, still fascinated at being able to *verbally* speak again.

Nereida looked at Viyan.

"Don't worry you'll get used to it, just answer the questions that you do remember," he laughed.

"Well, this is actually not the first time I am visiting this land," she answered. "As a child, I would sneak off and venture out into the seas and visit many lands. When my dad got tired of worrying about me disappearing, he assigned Eimear to look after me as I grew. I know of this place because I have been here before. But it is tricky because since it is hidden away, it is not always easy to find."

As Nereida spoke, Liam sensed the presence of something else close to them, although he didn't say anything. They continued to walk and while everyone was distracted in their conversations, Liam was on guard. He saw something from the corner of his eye but when he turned around, there was nothing there. "Did anyone see anything move on this side?" he asked as he pointed to his right. Everyone shook their heads but while looking at Liam, they heard a movement in the direction that he had pointed. They immediately drew back to face the direction that the noise came from. They gathered closer together and clutched onto their weapons. After encountering the type of creatures that they had witnessed in the ocean, they were not taking any chances.

Chapter Eight

Bigfoot and the Fae

~ Elam ~

They remained still to see if there was any more movement. It could have just been an animal, but Liam could sense animals, and this was not anything he was used to. It felt human too. Liam's senses suggested that it was a creature like him. *Another Lycan?* But this was too far from home, it could not possibly be one like him.

The leaves of the trees began to move and out emerged an enormous beast. It was completely covered in dark brown, fur-like hair. It resembled a gorilla, but it was three times the size and it stood more upright. Samara gasped loudly when she saw it.

"Not to be afraid," the creature said softly as it made its way out from behind the trees.

They observed its moves as it made its way toward them.

"Me is here for you," it clarified.

"To rescue or to eat?" Samara asked under her breath.

The creature came closer, "I take you to home of Fae, they is waiting for you."

It felt recognizable to Viyan; there was a familiar kindness about it.

"Hello Ms. Nereida," it greeted, bowing its head in her direction. Nereida greeted the creature and assured the Defenders that it was safe for them to go with him.

The creature led them further into the woods. He had gigantic feet that left huge tracks wherever he stepped, but he was very careful where he walked, trampling softly and slowly. With his large feet and hairy body, they all had a pretty good idea of who he was.

"What do we call you?" Catori asked as they walked behind him.

He turned around to answer, "My name Yayali is but humans call me as *Big Foot*."

"Well. They certainly weren't wrong," Samara commented, staring at his massive feet.

Yayali gently made his way through the woods until he got to a beautiful Oak tree with a huge tree trunk, way larger than the monster itself. The tree was magnificent, characterized by its unique form – a large trunk with outstretched twisted branches that appeared to extend to the sky. The tree stood out from the others, seemingly protected by the hawthorn and birch trees that surrounded it.

"I do not know if you have noticed but the trees that surround the magnificent Oak are found only around the Oak and nowhere else in this forest," Catori indicated as they approached the tree.

"We is here," Yayali said as he bent down to the oak tree bark.

Catori touched one of the birch tree's barks. "The birch is a significant tree, it represents new beginnings, wonder and adventure. But it also is a tree of protection against evil and negative energies. Whatever the birch and hawthorn protect, is within that tree." Catori pointed to the Oak.

Yayali was bent at the base of the Oak tree. He looked at them and then turned back around to the tree to whisper something foreign into the bark. Seconds later a crack began to form in it. The words, '*Afar oak, hi agh thorn (By Oak, Ash and Thorn)*' opened a small portal that began to grow in size until there was a complete pathway through the gigantic tree bark. Yayali squeezed himself through the tree opening and signaled for the others to follow before he made his way fully through.

"Why did you have to make it sound so ominous, Cat? Right before we are asked to follow through a path that did not exist 30 seconds ago," Samara said nervously.

Nereida held Samara's shoulder, "I trust Yayali, and you will soon understand why these protective trees surround the Oak." She held out her hand to Samara. "Trust me."

Samara placed her hand in Nereida's and they both followed Yayali through the tree.

One by one the others made their way through. It was about a 200-metre walk from the entrance to the exit. The light from the other end was bright and shone through to the inside of the trunk, guiding the way. The walkway formed a tunnel which was green all the way through and smelt of sweet, freshly cut grass. As they walked along, flowers began to sprout and bloom as though the tunnel was coming to life in their presence. When they exited the tunnel they walked out into a wide-open woodland space, but it was nothing like the forest they had just left from. The outside land was green and woody but the inside was colourful and animated.

They gasped with amazement at the scene, it was simply glorious. Lush and alive with an array of large, brightly coloured flora.

"This reminds me of Atlantis," Nereida complimented.

It did. It looked just like it in its glory of colour. Although, where Atlantis was more gold and had intense metallic shades, this was an indulgence of bright, rich colour. And the smell was sensational; floral, sweet and delicious. It was also rather busy, with large fluttering insects moving around, flying from flowers and trees. Among the movement was also conversation and laughter, but no other people were visible. The bustle instantaneously quieted down once they had all fully crossed through the tunnel.

Yayali continued to walk ahead through the pathed grass-way which formed beneath an avenue of trees. He made his way to a flat stoned circular patch on the ground a little way in and sat down. It seemed that it was his personal spot because overhead hung a shaded terrace of palm leaves and pretty bluebells with pink, white and yellow angel's trumpet growing through. Just enough to shade the big creature. The others followed Yayali to where he sat and as they walked, they saw troves of winged insects flying past them and toward him. The insects were holding up palm leaves with the freshest fruit inside. It was so strange to see, as if trained insects were little flying waiters.

"Ahhh, perhaps they are from a trained flea circus, you know, like the ones we used to watch in cartoons when we were kids," Samara tapped Viyan excitedly while suggesting this to him.

As the group walked closer to Yayali, brightly coloured toadstools began to pop up beside him under the terrace.

A gigantic toadstool was used as a table, and around the mushroom table, the coloured toadstools popped up for the five to sit on. The closer the Defenders got, the clearer they were able to see the winged insects. They were not insects at all but rather tiny humans with wings. They were the size of a male bee hummingbird and completely clothed. The five guests gawked with open mouths as the little flying people brought food to them.

"This is what I meant when I said that you will understand what the trees are there to protect," Nereida said, pointing to the hawthorn trees scattered throughout the landscape. "These hawthorns are the trees of the Fae; they house and keep them safe. However, it is also gateway to the fairy-world. That is exactly where you are now and these are the hosts of this world," she described as more fairies flew in.

The fairies hovered over in groups of four, holding up banana tree leaves with fruit and nuts and other foods. Some carried, in pairs, goblets made from bluebells filled with nectar, juice and water. Yayali gestured that the Defenders should eat the food prepared for them. They didn't need any convincing. They were famished and partook immediately. The fruit was delectable, sweet and juicy. The most delicious fruit they had ever tasted. The little people brought in more and more food as the Defenders rapidly consumed it. They carried in flowers of different shapes and sizes and each functioned as bowls holding purees and cooked fruits and vegetables. The food was inexplicably bursting with flavour. It was a gastronomical delight.

"It feels as though the food is dancing in my mouth," Catori complimented.

"A symphony of flavours!" Samara agreed. "Are you sure this is just fruit and vegetables?!" she asked the fairy waiters. *"No butter? No sugar?"*

They just smiled and flew off.

"I knew it!" she accused. "Nothing natural could ever taste this good!"

But it was natural. All natural. The produce was just grown in a happier, more loving climate. And it was that one small element which made all the difference. Well that, and the fact that Elam was a magical land. But it was mostly *love and happiness*.

"As delectable as the food is, I would just like to know where we are exactly," Samara queried, as she crammed the food into her mouth.

The others nodded with stuffed faces.

"Can you tell us a little about this place?" Viyan asked Yayali.

"This is hidden forest where Fae lives. Fae is peoples who protect *Yantra*."

Yayali was slow and soft-spoken. It was a calmer environment compared to when they had met him and so they now noticed his speech. He had a deep yet warm tone. Before they could ask for any more information, they noticed a commotion in the surrounding trees up ahead. As the movement neared, they first heard soft music playing and then the sound of trumpets blared, as if to announce someone's arrival.

A cute baby elephant waddled toward them making its way from the trees onto the pathway in front of them. Across its back lay a mat made of leaves and straw, and hovering above this was a single tulip. The flower resembled an umbrella, a pastel pink parrot tulip, held up with its stalk by little fairies. The elephant came closer to them and then stopped a short distance away. A few of the petals of the flower lifted open like a curtain being drawn and a fairy creature flew slowly out of the flower in which it had been resting. Yayali bowed to the fairy and the elephant blew his trunk like a trumpet, announcing a royal arrival. This little creature flew from the flower and rested on the mat on the elephant's back. Then, right in front of everyone's eyes, it began to grow spontaneously in size, until it was a few centimetres taller than Viyan, who was the tallest of the Defenders. Everyone stared in bemusement at this marvel. The fairy had grown into a young man, dressed in a pure white pants and a white shirt. He wore a crown made from beautiful, colourful flowers entwined with delicate golden ropes, and in his hand he held a staff made from stalks and leaves. At the top of the staff sat an emerald-coloured stone.

Some fairy folk flew in with a goblet of water for the royal to drink. He took a sip and then looked up at them. "*Parched!*" he exclaimed somewhat out of breath. "It always takes a lot out of me when I change in size," he said in eloquent speech. The elephant seemed as though its legs were about to buckle at the weight of its passenger, and so the young man jumped off immediately.

"Sorry there, Duke!" the man apologised to the elephant as he patted it on its head. "Just thought I would make a little bit of an entrance for our guests," he mentioned to the group with a chuckle.

The young man moved over to the group and sat on a toadstool that popped up magically at the table next to them. He was very well-spoken.

"I am Prince Caden, welcome to our home. We are elated that you have arrived."

The Prince was handsome with sunkissed skin, bright blue-green eyes and golden-blonde hair. And his accent made him ever so more appealing. The other thing that stood out, apart from his attractive looks, were his ears which were pointed at the tip. He caught Catori staring at them.

"And these things, he said as he swooped his almost shoulder-length hair to the side with a flick of his head, these are what makes me Fae. All of us who live here are Fae. We are fairies and pixies and elves all living happily and harmoniously in our home which we call, Elam." As these words left the Prince's lips, suddenly, out of nowhere these very creatures began to appear; elves, fairies and pixies. They came out of hiding within the trees and surroundings and when they did, the forest itself began to sink away and an entire city emerged. It was as if the forest that the Defenders walked into was an illusion. The tall grass and trees began to part, revealing a bright and colourful, energetic forest of wonder. Trees in various shades of green with fresh, ripe fruit hanging from most, formed the foundation of the forest and everything developed around it. Wooden huts on the ground and in the trees began to appear, and the bustling noise that they heard when they first arrived began again.

Animals and insects appeared, strange and familiar ones. Brightly feathered peacocks walked about, illuminating the landscape. Some had feathers which were the traditional rich blues, greens and yellows and then some whose feathers were pastel and neon shades roamed freely. Birds of different sizes and various colours flew about. Tropical dodos and toucans shared each other's company as they flew around. Baby elephants, baby cheetahs and little buck were seen in the far distance, playing among the trees. The colours of the creatures were vibrant and luminous. All stood out, unique in their appearance.

The Defenders spotted a frogmouth whose feathers looked like a whisper of resting emperor moths. A beautiful bird with royal blue, fine, fur-like feathers which filtered down into what resembled a trail of a wedding dress held at the head by an elegant, crown-like laced crest, traipsed gracefully past them. A blue-black feathered pigeon, whose plumage from the neck down was tropical shades of greens, blues and oranges twirled by and its feathers opened in imitation of a ballerina whose colourful tutu captured everyone's attention. These creatures seemed to have personalities of their own.

As the Prince introduced these forest wonders, a comical-looking chubby, spotted guinea fowl, with a beak almost as big as the bird itself, shuffled on a low-lying tree branch in an attempt to fly off of it. It stretched out its wings to display disproportionately small appendages. The bird made its way to the edge of the branch ready to fly but instead merely fell off. It picked itself up ready to try again. The Defenders were amused by the cute entertainment. In the distraction, they were caught off guard by a sizeable bird which swooped in low, right past them, only to land on a high tree branch nearby. The judgmental Eurasian eagle-owl, with its pointed ears and flame-orange eyes, perched on the branch watchfully.

The Fae, as introduced by Prince Caden, were just as varied as everything else in the forest. Creatures similar looking to humans but with some noticeable differences appeared in various sizes and forms. Tiny little folk with wings flew around the flowers and through the trees as more stout looking folk muddled about with some slender, taller ones. Both types were very much human looking but had slightly pointed ears at the helix and while the shorter ones had slightly more mature faces, the taller ones had youthful, angelic features.

"The pixies are the ones with wings and can communicate with plant life. They are responsible for the vibrance in Elam. The fairies have the magical ability to transform in size and appearance. We can fly with the pixies or walk with the elves, and you can tell us apart because we fairies have glow about us. The elves do not have this glow as they are the most human looking and the ones most able to connect with humans. They also cannot transform as the fairies can." The Prince looked admirably on at the folk of Elam as they went about their business.

"I am not sure if you know this but we Fae are as old as the Earth herself. When she was created, we were asked to care for her. Our purpose as the Fae was always to protect the Earth and her beautiful creations. Helping her form and sustain life, we cared for the plant and animal beings. But, when the World changed and much of the natural creations were destroyed, our lives and roles on Earth were threatened. Thus, we brought what we could into a space where we would be able to protect the Earth as we were purposed to. This is the Elam that you are now in."

The Prince talked them through life on Elam. He explained that while it is hidden today, it was not always so. Much of the Earth was just as beautiful and magical as Elam, but because of the slow destruction many of the once magnificent creatures went extinct. When the Fae decided to move to a land away from all the chaos, Elam was formed. At the creation of Elam, the inhabitants used to live freely without any boundaries and everyone lived harmoniously, even the humans who chose to share the space with them. There were many other Guardians who once lived with the Fae, including the Shamanic people and the Lycan. But it was eventually decided that they all had to go separate ways for their own protection, and for the greater protection of the Earth. Some of the humans who lived among the Fae became jealous of their magic and powers and the same as with the other Guardians, they began to create stories about them being mischievous. As the stories grew, they depicted the Fae as evil and malevolent, and the younger generations of humans eventually tried to destroy them out of fear.

When the Guardians who had retreated to different parts of the Earth began to experience the same threat, the Fae withdrew deeper into their forest and created a protection spell around it, restricting human contact. The Fae were more than capable of defending themselves as they were very powerful, but they were also a peaceful race and did not seek to fight. They were sent to Earth to protect Her, and their greatest purpose was to keep safe the secret emulate Yantra. Yantra, the most powerfully contained magic on Earth, was destined to be the sacred activator that would save the Earth at the time of the battle. When the Fae secretly locked away their home, Yayali vowed to keep their barriers safe.

The Prince turned to Viyan. "We are so glad that you have returned as you said you would."

Viyan whose face grew from contentment to confusion, shook his head.

"Great! Another life that I don't remember!"

"Did you never wonder why you had such pointy ears?" The Prince laughed as he touched the tip of Viyan's ears.

"Well, now that you mention it, I always did," Samara replied, nodding her head and giggling.

The Prince turned to look at her, "Princess Xaria, I take it that you too do not recall your stay here?"

Samara immediately stopped her chuckling and turned to look directly at the Prince. That name was awfully familiar. It was the name her mother had given to her in secret, a name that no one else besides her family knew.

"*How do you know that name*?!" she asked him.

"There once was a time when you lived as a princess in the outer world. But you were very much a people's princess who did not care about title or wealth, so you did not feel like you belonged to that royal world. After much seeking and guidance, you learnt of us Fae and came to find meaning here in Elam. You spent some time with us, learning ways to help your people lead a better life. It was at that same period that Viyan had come to live with us."

While Samara was processing this information, Prince Caden turned back to Viyan. "When you had left Atlantis, you came to Elam to live among us for a few years. Actually, not too many lifetimes before this current one. You then went on to live with the Lycans and then the Shamanic people to study more about human life and to gain knowledge from all the Guardian tribes for your mission. Your name, Viyan, means *special knowledge.* This is because you have gained the knowledge across many lifetimes for this very life that you live now. You possess all the knowledge needed to protect the Earth," the Prince assured Viyan with a tap on his shoulder.

Viyan rubbed his ears, but he could not seem to remember this life. *How could he possibly have gained all the knowledge needed and what was the point if he could not remember it?* All of these things that he was learning about himself did not seem real. But at the same time, how was any of this real; standing in an enchanted forest, having visited the mythical Atlantis, saving the World from a catastrophic threat? Just a few days ago he was managing a store, living a normal happy life with his friends. Nothing out of the ordinary, just a simple pleasant life with no inclination to any of this craziness. And he was happy and content. Now he was travelling to foreign places – extremely foreign, so foreign that they were previously unfound – meeting warriors and discovering the existence of legendary creatures. *How is any of it even real?*

"I am sure that none of this is making sense to you," the Prince said to Viyan, picking up on the doubt and confusion. "It must seem strange and unbelievable and perhaps even far-fetched."

"Yes! None of this seems real. None of it makes any sense," Samara interrupted.

"We were average kids, living average lives just a few days ago. And now .... well, I don't even know. In a few days, our lives have been completely flipped over. I no longer know what is real anymore." Samara was thrown off course by the information of a past life. It was ok when it was happening to Viyan because she did not have to make sense of it first-hand, but now that it was her turn, it was different.

It's hard enough to deal with one life but now I have to deal with another, she thought to herself.

"Cat and Liam grew up with this knowledge but this was suddenly sprung on Viyan and me. Even though we just went through all this craziness, it is still a little difficult to comprehend."

"I have grown up with these stories and it is still hard for me to make sense of what I have just been through," Liam said, trying to comfort her.

"Oh! But you are so much more than just average! You have always been!" the Prince said admirably. "This was the plan. You were just bidding time till the moment was right. This was always meant to happen, and you have been preparing for it through lifetimes. You were born into this and what you call an *average life* was so for a reason. By you not remembering anything, it was so that you would have been protected and safe until the time came for you to resume your mission."

Prince Caden paused to think. "Follow me,' he said. "Hopefully this will provide more clarity."

~ The Knowing ~

Prince Caden led the group through the forest, with Duke plodding after them. He walked them across the lush green foliage, through a pathway which was not there at first but that formed in front of him as he walked. The forest was bustling with creatures, but they all became still as the Prince passed. The flowers also shifted aside to make way. The forest's aroma was a beautiful floral scent that switched between sweet and citrus. A peaceful energy flowed throughout making the walk calming and healing. No one felt the need to say anything.

Down the walkway, they reached a small lake with a waterfall falling into it. A little gorge formed between rocks covered in grass and splashes of colourful flowers. However, the waterfall's source was not visible. The water rather fell from light, fluffy white clouds, into the river. It was still and calm like the forest itself and it provided the base of the river that ran through Elam. This setting was recognisable to both Viyan and Samara but they were not sure how they knew it. As they got closer, they saw a magnificent tree and realised why the scene was familiar. This was the place from their visions.

Viyan turned to Samara. "Does this look …" before he could finish asking Samara replied, "Yup" while nodding her head in amazement. "It sure is … dreamlike."

They had come full circle from where this adventure had started.

"Viyan, why don't you take a seat under the tree," Prince Caden suggested.

Viyan took a walk to the tree and sat below it. He instinctively closed his eyes and entered into a meditative state. He did not even know that he could mediate, it was not something he had done before this experience. It was just an automatic response to the tree. The others decided to take a walk to admire the surrounding beauty while they waited for Viyan. Little fairies and small creatures flying around grabbed their attention and they followed them. The tree began to lower one of its branches and offered Viyan tiny fruit enclosed within pods. Small berry-like fruit that resembled red, shiny apples, the same as the fruit of the hawthorn tree. The branch reached Viyan's shoulder and with closed eyes, he plucked the fruits off the branch and bit into them, as he had done with the apple in his vision. And just like before, the sweetest, juice coated the back of his throat sending a soothing sensation through his body.

Viyan entered a deeper meditative state and visualized Durga once again. He felt Her intense yet calming energy on his skin. She was walking toward him in a clear space and as a warm wind breezed past, it caused Her luscious locks to flow back. It was as if She was crossing unseen barriers to get to him - an invisible dimensional space. Again, She was accompanied by the lion. The Goddess came up to Viyan and Her companion brushed up familiarly against him. Durga stood in front of Viyan and gave him a friendly comforting smile. She extended her arm and offered him a flower. It was a beautiful, richly fragrant *lotus*. As he raised the flower to his nose, he instantaneously began to get flashes of his past. But not just this life, all of his past lives. His brain began to download visual information of lives he had lived and lessons he had learnt. Flashes of who he used to be passed through his mind; the people he lived with and the places he had called home. Information that he did not know before had now become a part of his memory.

When the visions stopped, still in the meditative state, Durga came back to him. "I remember it all! It's like déjà vu but I don't feel anything. As the memories rushed through my mind, I remembered all the times, but there was just no emotional connection to them!" Viyan exclaimed, aware of so much now.

"You are sitting under the *Tree of Life*. It connects the Spiritual realm with the Earthly realm and symbolises the connection to everything. This is why I can meet you here," Durga explained. "It is also the representation of eternal life, and why you have learnt about your *immortality*," She elaborated. "Your soul is immortal. As humans, you are constantly evolving, this is what it is to be human – to experience, to learn and to grow. *Lifetimes* are for this reason, to develop and learn and become better. However, in every lifetime you change, and as you get older you sometimes cannot relate to the person you used to be. The reason that you have no emotional connection to those people that you used to be, is because you are no longer them - you have evolved and grown. But this does not mean that you did not learn from who you once were. Those lessons are what you keep with you. It is what you have accumulated over lifetimes and is what has helped you flourish. It has made you who you are today."

Now that he remembered those lessons, Viyan could understand what the Goddess meant.

"Within a lifetime humans accumulate lessons which help them personally evolve. They reflect on these lessons as memories. You can reflect on these lessons and learnings across all of your lifetimes. It does not change who you are now, it is just meant to help you on the mission."

Durga reiterated how the different lives that Viyan had lived was a training for his current life. His youth was his advantage in terms of stamina and strength but the knowledge and wisdom that he carried in his soul was ancient. All the Guardians had lifetimes of knowledge embedded within them, knowledge which could be unleashed when needed.

Durga enlightened Viyan on the next part of their journey. She confirmed that they would be going to *Africa* and that it was there that they would fight for Earth's survival. The *heart of the Earth* was in Africa. It was once the cradle of life and the richest site on the planet. Because the Earth was in pain, that heart-center had become the weakest point over the years. Since time was precious, Durga would help as much as She could for them to get to Africa, but was restricted from getting too involved. Elam was protected and so She could visit them there but otherwise, it was too risky. "One more thing," the Goddess said to Viyan as he was leaving his meditative state. "I think you left someone behind at the start of this journey. He is ready to accompany you the rest of the way." She rubbed her companion on the head before he walked away and out of the vision.

Viyan regained awareness. He looked around but no one was there. *They must have left*, he thought. It felt as if so much time had passed but it had only been 15 minutes. What seemed like hours to him was just minutes to the others exploring the surroundings. They returned and huddled eagerly around him as he described what he had visualised.

"I was given so much of information, things I could not have possibly known." He turned to his sister. "For instance, the fruit from that tree," he said, pointing to the tree he had just sat under "… is protected within a winged pod called a *samara*. How could I possibly know that?"

He smiled at her, "I also just know that that is exactly who you are, *A Protector.*"

Viyan was interrupted by a rustle among the trees. They all stepped back watching the nearby bushes as the leaves began to move. It certainly was not a tiny creature. They heard a sound and saw the rapid movement through the trees as if something was running at them. Even the Prince was alarmed. The creature drew close and as it ran out of the nearby bush everyone sighed a huge relief.

"Simha!" Samara shouted as she knelt to hug the dog.

Simha walked over to Viyan and brushed up against his leg. Viyan instinctively knew who his true form was.

"How did you get here?" Samara asked.

"He was sent to us," Viyan responded as he patted the dog.

The Prince, who had been standing at the bank of the river, walked over to where the group stood. "You should spend the night and rest well before you venture off on the next leg of your journey," he advised. "But before we head back something is waiting for Samara."

Samara raised her eyebrows, unsure if she heard correctly. "*Me?!*" she shouted excitedly.

"Your gift seems to be behind the waterfall," Prince Caden said with a smile.

They turned to look at the waterfall but could not see anything at first. Then they noticed a shimmer behind the fall, but still, there was nothing physically there. Suddenly, a rainbow of bright light struck behind it. Still no movement.

"Do I need to go into the water?" Samara asked nervously.

As she asked this, the falls parted and a magnificent white horse with a long shimmering mane slowly stepped out through it. The water connected again behind the equine, closing the gap. When the horse had completely emerged from behind the fall and the rainbow of light disappeared, they could see a shimmering pearl-like horn on his forehead.

"*A unicorn!*" Samara squealed with delight. The unicorn slowly walked toward them through the shallow waters of the forest pool. It then stepped out, onto the bank and walked up to Samara where it bowed its head to her.

"Meet Tarquin, your companion. Born from the waters of Elam, Tarquin is the purest and most magical of us all. He represents the best of the Earth and even carries some of Her spirit. He is made of magic and love and was created just for you. He is …"

But before the Prince could finish, Samara walked toward Tarquin and with a smile gently said, "My weapon."

Samara placed her hand on the unicorn's bowed head and whispered, "Hello Quinn. I cannot believe that after all these years, you truly are real."

Samara had had many dreams of this very same unicorn when she was growing up, and she knew that it was him the minute that she looked into his eyes. She felt an instant rush of energy move throughout her body. Thrilled with the reality, and relieved that her belief in unicorns for all these many years was not a childish fantasy – that unicorns really did exist - Samara was overjoyed by the realisation that he existed just for her.

"Tarquin actually is not your weapon," the Prince explained once Samara had acquainted herself with the unicorn. "He is your companion. However, he does have your special weapon with him."

Wrapped around Quinn's waist was a belt and to the side rested a katana within a holster. Samara drew out the beautiful sword from the holster. With a handle made from unicorn horn and a blade carved with the markings of a lion, it was a stunning piece. She touched the sword and a surge of energy flowed through her as she connected with her weapon. Samara smiled to herself, feeling everything falling purposefully into place.

"Let us head back to the castle," the Prince said to gather the others up, giving Samara a moment to herself. "You will spend the night there with us to rest yourselves before heading back on your journey."

They followed the Prince back through the forest to his little castle. It had grown darker as the sun began to set. As they walked through the woodlands, they could see the castle in the distance. It was concealed by a lot of foliage and tall trees. The castle was closer to the falls than it was to the village. Running alongside it was a small stream which flowed back to the river.

"I can feel that there is much power contained in these waters," Nereida said as she held her hand over the river, absorbing its energy.

"The waters in this stream and the greater river are very powerful as this is what sustains the magic in Elam," Prince Caden confirmed.

"Did anyone else notice how dark it has suddenly gotten?" Samara asked as she joined them. "Does Elam have its own sun?"

"Not as such," the Prince responded. "While Elam is its own domain, it is closed off from the outside world only by access. Everything in here is still living and very much a part of the Earth, thus we need the sun to grow. Think of this place as invisible; just because we cannot be seen, it does not mean that we do not exist," he explained, confusing Samara even more.

The castle was made out of natural white marble stone and covered in creepers, vines and flowers. It was a beautiful structure that grew from the forest rather than having been built. The palace, while magnificent in design and structure, was not so in size. It was much too small for them to enter.

"Ahhh, I foresee a tiny problem here. You are not tiny and that is the problem," the Prince said sheepishly, already knowing this before he invited them over. He pulled out a small canister from the satchel that he carried. He dipped it into the stream to collect some water. Prince Caden asked them each, one by one, to take a sip of the water from the canister. As he did so, in swooped the judgmental owl from earlier in the day. He startled them all. The owl flew in and sat on one of the branches of the large tree that grew beside the river.

"That is ever so ominous," Samara said, spooked by the owl who stared down at them.

Samara looked at Viyan as if to ask, *Are you sure it is ok to drink?*

He smiled back at her and nodded his head to say, *Yes*.

First Viyan took a sip, followed by Samara then Catori, Nereida and finally Liam. The Prince bent to give Simha some water too. After they had sipped the water, which had a pure, crisp, cool taste, Prince Caden began to recite some words in Fae. He raised his hands and head to the sky, closed his eyes and uttered, "Nha Al alura aul Tel' drii, nha Al alura aul tel'quiet. Sen ary, Quor'She Kyed nha wee (*There is a change in the air, there is a change in me. What once was big, now is wee*)."

As the last word left his lips, a slight breeze cut the still air. It was followed by a whirlwind of warm current which rustled the trees. They felt the wind pass them by and saw it moving onto the water, causing slight waves to form in the stream. Once the wind subsided, they slowly saw each other starting to decrease in size. Now smaller versions of themselves, they were roughly half of the sizes that they used to be. They tried to make sense of the transformation by studying their new physiques. Each looking at their hands, arms and legs before turning to examine the changes in each other.

"Well, I always wanted a mini-me," Samara said positively.

Liam nudged Catori, "Guess this makes you a kitten."

Catori raised her eyebrows and huffed. She looked straight ahead of her, ignoring him.

"Guess this gives you a reason for always behaving like a child."

There was silence and then they all roared with laughter.

Liam smiled and nodded his head approvingly, "Ouch! Nice one Cat!"

Although they had changed in size, because their weapons were magical, they could not be altered in form.

The Prince had to cast a protection spell to hide them in the river where they would be guarded for the night. He muttered another incantation and the weapons lifted off from the ground. An iridescent bubble formed around them and they moved over the water and then lowered into the stream. Prince Caden changed back to a smaller size and walked the Defenders to his castle. Quinn stayed beside the river keeping watch over the weapons while the others retired to the castle for the night.

~ Chateau de Colores ~

The castle was still rather small despite their now mini-er forms. It was the size of a simple duplex 4-bedroom home. But when they stepped inside, they were once again transported to a different space. Everything on this journey had been so elusive.

"What in the …" Samara yelled when she saw the never-ending space on the inside. It was enormous! "This is what I imagined life to be like for my Barbies," she lamented, as she thought back to her childhood.

When she was younger, Samara's active imagination would have her think about what her Barbies would get up to at night once she had tucked them into their doll house beds. She would dream that they would have *girls' night* every night as she pictured Barbie and her friends driving their convertible through the house halls.

The castle's walls were white marble with accents of different colours that continuously changed. The lines in the marble subtly changed from amethyst to quartz to emerald to aquamarine and tigers-eye. There was a lot of activity on the inside as a few elves and fairies carried about items as if preparing for a festivity of sorts. The Prince invited his guests to freshen up and asked them to meet for dinner an hour later in the dining hall. Each was then led to their own rooms by a host. Staircases in the main hall led to a floor above where the rooms were situated. Each host headed for a staircase, followed by their guest. As they walked up the stairs the cases began to shuffle. The stairs switched position as the pairs made their way up, each staircase carrying them directly to the landing outside their rooms. The staircases guided each Guardian to the room meant for them and the doors automatically opened, revealing the rooms' unique luminescent colour.

Every room had an oak bed and oak furniture, with fresh flowers emitting a unique scent. Samara's room was *lilac* and decorated with *amethyst* crystals placed around on the furniture. A bouquet of *lilies*, her favourite flower, immediately relaxed her when she entered. A *turquoise* shade of blue brightened Nereida's room along with the *aquamarine* crystals placed around it. Mid-blue and bluish-purple *hyacinths* decorate the space while a *peppermint* scent filled the air. Catori's room was covered in various shades of *greens* - from pine to jade to Persian and earthy - with *emerald* crystals distributed around the area. Potted pink *orchids* as well as small bouquets of pink *carnations* were placed around her room while a *rose* aroma flattered the setting.

Viyan's room was shaded *royal blue* with varying *hydrangea* bouquets bringing through the colours of Atlantis. A large hexagonal *sodalite* crystal, surrounded by smaller ones were placed on a mirror table. The crystals were symbolic of the vast universe. His room had a spicey yet woody smell of *palo santo*. Liam's room was coloured with shades of grey and decorated with *bloodstone* - black stone with specs of red and brown, reminiscent of the dark night and the blood moon. Arabian night *dahlias* and dark-red oriental *stargazers* filled his room along with a *sandalwood* scent.

Their baths had been drawn for them in tubs fashioned out of giant tulips. The water was soothing and cleansing and the soak made a world of difference, relaxing and rejuvenating them.

Time seemed to move slower in Elam. They were given some space to absorb the energy of their individually allocated rooms, till each heard a knock at their doors. Their escorts were there to take them down to the dining hall. Each Defender stepped out of their room wearing white cotton pants and cotton-sleeved tops. It was soft, light and cool and complimented the ambience of the castle. They all simultaneously headed down their staircases for dinner and were led into the banquet hall by their guides.

The hall was a spacious room with stone floors and just a long 10-seater table, constructed out of tree bark, in the middle. The table and chairs were beautifully carved, with intricate pattern work. The wall on the right side of the room had six large arch windows that looked onto the stream outside. The stream acted as a natural source of luminance as the moonlight reflected off its waters and out into the beautifully manicured lush green garden. Fireflies lit up the area with their beams of fluttering light. The lighting within the room felt natural too, but it fell from the chandeliers which hung from the ceiling.

When they entered the banquet hall, the Prince was already seated at the table. He alerted the kitchen as soon as they walked into the room. The chairs automatically moved away from the table so that the guests could take a seat. They were then gently pushed toward the table and the cotton napkin on their plates unfolded on its own and moved to lay across their laps. Fresh flowers fell from the ceiling, releasing a gorgeous welcoming floral scent. They looked up to admire the soft glow from above. It was the moon. The ceiling was the night sky, but it was not an open roof, nor a glass ceiling, nor painted on. The moving night sky sat in place of the ceiling, complete with stars and light clouds flying slowly across. The chandeliers were vines that grew below the ceiling to midway down the length of the hall. Fresh flowers were constantly blooming on the vines and light emitted from brightly glowing fireflies sitting on the vines. Birds could be heard chirping along with the soft sound of a waterfall in the distant background. Perhaps the waterfall could be heard because of the stillness of the night, but it was strange to hear birds chirping so late.

"Is it just me or is that painting moving?" Samara asked fearfully.

They all turned toward the wall opposite of the windows. The entire wall was a beautiful mural with a vivid, very realistic-looking recreation of the waterfall and its surroundings. As they stared at it, a fish jumped out of the water and dived back in, and as it did, droplets of water sprayed onto them. Birds flew from time to time, from one tree to another, rustling the leaves on the trees. The painting was as alive as Elam itself.

Formally dressed Fae walked in with trays full of food. The setting was more formal at dinner than at lunch, and it was fancier. The food was laid out on wooden trays, instead of leaves. The glasses were elegant flower flutes with long green stems and their plates were large, pressed, glossed-over flowers. Their cutlery was carved out of wood, not that it was needed. And the food! Although just a mix of fresh fruit and cooked vegetables, it smelt spectacular. Nereida was not used to such types of food, but she enjoyed it most of all.

"It's not fish ... but it's so tasty," she expressed as she took her first bite.

They ate heartily and the conversation was just as enriching.

"So, this where you live? In the castle? And is this your life?" Samara asked. "If so, let me just say, WOW!" she continued without giving the Prince a chance to answer.

"Yes. And no," he replied with a smile. "I do live in the castle for formality, but it is never like this. We have made it formal for you. Otherwise, it is usually a small, informal dwelling. I do have a chef to prepare meals for me because, despite all the magic, I have never been good at cooking," he admitted. "But anyone is welcome at any time. I am outside in the village with the rest of the Fae anyway. It is not so formal anymore," he paused. "It feels really nice to have the castle alive again, just like when I was little. Every night used to be special like this," he continued, as he looked around. He imagined the castle as it was years ago when he was little. He recalled the feasts and the dances that would take place. He remembered how he would run through the halls with the other young ones and pass through the banquet room where he would catch his parents lovingly dancing together. So many fond memories of a happier time.

"Elam is a vibrant, happy place, but there was a time when it was so much more … of everything," Prince Caden remarked. He talked about how the running of Elam had changed and why. With a sad tone, he explained why he had to oversee its management. "My parents ruled a very happy kingdom and the people loved them. They were not the Queen and King but just folk of Elam and even lived among the other Fae. Rule is a strong word. Our royal responsibility is to preserve the peace and structure and to ensure that the Fae follow through with our purpose. Mostly, we had to protect the sacred stone through generations, always knowing that this time would come. Our main objective, apart from protecting the stone, was to protect the Earth." He exhaled heavily. "When I was born, my parents created this castle knowing that I would one day have to take over from them. They wanted me to be protected if anything ever happened to them. We have had numerous threats on the kingdom because of the stone of course. But the protection spells on our kingdom came from very strong magic and the joy and love that radiated from the Fae only strengthened that magic. But when the time grew closer to the prophecy, the folk of Elam began to worry. They became more fearful and as a result, the protective magic began to weaken."

The Prince paused to take a sip of his drink and then he explained the source of their power. "The Fae were never influenced by the negative qualities that plagued Man. The effects of greed and power that led to the demise of humans never entered our kingdom. Fae magic came from a place of purity. The magic was based on intuition and belief, there was never any doubt in what we did nor in who we were, and thus there was purity in our magic. The Fae did not have to worry about competition; everyone was equal. Even though we as royals lived in the castle, it was open to anyone who wanted to come here. There was no control and the Fae, up to today, do not feel that I am superior in any way. They respect me but perhaps that is because I have only their best interests at heart, as did all my forefathers before me."

He took another sip before ending his story.

"I said that we never were influenced by any negativity before. However, once the Fae began to feel fear, it spread quickly till the collective began to feel fearful. This was the first time that this happened to us and because the purity inside Elam was tainted, the strength of our magic weakened.

My parents and the Elders grew concerned that Elam and the Fae would be at risk. Some of our Elam family along with my parents left home to protect it from the outside."

Prince Caden let out a heavy sigh. "Because of all the changes in the world, greed and ego were on the rise, my parents realised that this would lead to a significant increase in portals, allowing negative creatures onto Earth. And so, they left Elam to try to stop the destruction. Yayali was asked to stay and guard the woods around Elam. That is why he roams the outer forest and comes home from time to time. I have tried my best to run the kingdom, but I am no comparison to them."

Nereida placed her hand on Prince Caden's, "It is not easy to run a kingdom but from what I can see, your parents would be so proud." She smiled a smile of assurance.

"Thank you," he replied.

The tension was eased when more food was brought in.

"Ahhh, dessert!" the Prince exclaimed, trying to brighten the mood.

"We know how you love your sweet treats, so our chef had been practising how to make pie," he said excitedly. Delicious dessert dishes were brought to the table; pumpkin, apple, cherry and banana pie, among many others. As stuffed as they all were, they devoured the pies. They were unlike any they had ever tasted. Undoubtedly, as with everything else, there was magic in every bite.

Before the end of the evening, the Prince shared with them where they would be heading to next and explained how they would get to their final destination. Time was of the essence and because that destination was on an entirely different continent, they would need some fairy-magic to get them there. The Defenders would have to go back through the Enchanted Tree to exit into the forest of their desired location.

"Where exactly is this destination?" Samara asked.

"Home," Viyan replied. "*Africa!*"

There was a pause and a little silence as a warm rush coursed through Samara's body. She had often dreamed of being back in Africa since she was a little girl. The memories of her home were distant, but her dreams were fresh. She always thought they were just very vivid dreams, but she now realized that they were *callings*.

"Well, you need to get your rest because the toughest part of your journey lies ahead," the Prince advised. They left the dining hall and returned to their rooms to rest. And it was the most peaceful of sleeps they had ever had. Soothed by the most beautiful dreams, they woke up refreshed and well-rested.

At 5 a.m., the sun peered through Samara's room curtain and woke her. And for the first time, she didn't mind waking up at the crack of dawn.

Just then a fairy helper flew into the room to draw the curtains open.

"Good morning miss," the little lady said to her.

"Great morning!" Samara chirped back.

Each of the Defenders were awakened by the sunlight entering their rooms. After bathing, when they stepped back into their chambers, a new outfit awaited them on their beds. The outfits that they arrived in had been fashioned for an individual fit, each one now wearing the shade matching that of their room.

Things were less formal that morning with no aid guiding them around. Once Samara changed, she walked down to the banquet room for breakfast. As she headed down the stairs, she saw Nereida.

"Morning. How did you sleep?" she called to Nereida from her staircase.

"Good morning! I had the most wonderful rest," Nereida shouted back from hers.

The group was seated at the dining table when the two walked in.

"Good morning," the Prince greeted them.

"Good morning, Sire," Samara said as she joined the table.

The night ceiling was now the morning sky and the room was brightly lit. Samara sat at the table, with the view of the stream outside. As she looked at the garden, she saw Quinn grazing at the stream bed. It was indeed a glorious morning.

Just as with dinner, breakfast was brought with such gusto, and in mass loads. There was fresh fruit and pancakes and cakes and things they had never seen before. Simha was already tucking into some of the tasty food served to him beside the table on a wooden tray laid on the stone floor. The Defenders dished food onto their plates, sampling all the new delicacies. The Prince spoke, "I must say, you all look very dashing in your new clothes."

"Yes, we did not thank you for our wonderful surprise this morning," Liam replied.

"You are most welcome! A simple upgrade to the suits that you arrived in. Not only is it cool for the heat from the

African sun, but it is also warm if you have to encounter any cold or windy conditions. Not forgetting to mention, it is pretty stylish too. The colours are uniquely yours. Each shade aligns with the precious gemstones that represent and protect you only." He was very chuffed with the suits.

"The best part is that it is protected by magic. And not just any magic but the best of the best magic," he said excitedly.

He looked out onto the garden. "I am not sure if I mentioned this, but while all of the Fae are magical creatures, we have different magical capabilities, and some may be more gifted than others. Our Chief of magic is the most gifted of all the Fae, even I. Perhaps you have heard his name before. *Merlin?*" the Prince asked.

Samara almost choked on her drink. "*Merlin … the magician?*"

"How are you even surprised anymore!?" Viyan exclaimed.

"Yes, the same one. You may have seen him around – the big owl that keeps flying in on us at times. That's him!" the Prince clarified. "He re-designed and re-created your battle suits and there is magic in each fiber. It may not seem so because of its comfort." The Prince paused. "I know! Eat up and I will show you."

They made their way to the stream to gather their weapons before heading to the village. Outside at the stream, Quinn was resting beside the riverbed where he had been guarding the weapons overnight. "Are we ready?" Prince Caden asked.

He closed his eyes and raised his head and hands to the sky before saying, "Sarash ni- once kesha, Quor'She Kyed, back lor, nae ary eath'she more (Turned small once a time before, now back to big ever more).” A breeze rustled the trees and then a whirlwind of leaves, the size of a large twister for their reduced frames, consumed them as it passed by. A brief spin and they were thrown out, landing on the ground. But when they gently hit the ground, they had returned to normal size. As they landed, Prince Caden too transformed into his normal human size.

“Did that have to happen just after the massive breakfast that we ate?” Liam asked, feeling nauseated. “I am just trying to prepare you as best as I can for battle,” Prince Caden joked. He closed his eyes and raised his hands over the water. Waves formed and then the weapons began to rise out of the stream. The water slowly carried the weapons out of the river and onto the bank where the Defenders stood. They each bent down to collect their weapons and Samara, carrying her Katana, walked over to Quinn to greet him.

“Why is it that you did not have to say any incantation to remove the weapons from out of the water?” Catori asked as she walked over to the Prince.

“I have natural magic that does not need the use of spells. When I use the elements of nature, of the Earth, I do not always need to cite any incantation. However, when it comes to other creatures, I have to use an invocation to support my magical intent,” he explained.

“Makes sense,” Catori said with a nod as she thought about the logic.

“Right, now for the best part. Liam, could I use your sword for a minute please?”

Liam handed the Prince his sword without any question. Prince Caden accepted it with a smile and thanked Liam just before using it to stab him. Everyone went into complete shock, not knowing how to react. Liam froze, entirely surprised by the Prince's action. But when he realised that he had felt no pain, he looked down at his body and saw that the sword did not penetrate his suit. The Prince handed the sword back to a still dumbfounded Liam.

"Sorry for the element of surprise. But this is a lesson to never let your guard down and not to be too trusting of anyone." He paused. "Well, that, and to show you how utterly amazing these suits are," he continued excitedly. "They are impenetrable by any weapon or fire. You are completely protected. But …" the Prince took a deep breath in before continuing. "…these creatures feed off fear and all things negative. You have to remain strong and do not stop believing in yourself. You need to remain confident and positive to reinforce the magic of the suits." Again the Prince paused. Not wanting to lower the morale he continued, "We know that you will honour us all. You were all chosen for a reason. We believe in you, and you carry the blessings and support of not only the gods but of the Fae and all the extended Guardians."

Yayali met them at the stream and in his hand he carried a *club*. He was joining them in the battle. Samara smiled at him and gave him a nod and a wink. She remembered the weapon from her visions. Doing a quick mental check, she counted the weapons from the dream in which Durga revealed them. *Trident, spear, bow and arrow, sword, conch and mace.* There were still two weapons unaccounted for. It seemed that they were not done gathering Guardians.

Prince Caden delineated how they would return on their journey. They would make their way through the tree, the same way that they had entered Elam and would return out into the forest, or rather the wilderness, of Africa. Yayali would accompany them the rest of the way to assist and to protect the stone.

"Now. For *Yantra*!"

Once again, Prince Caden closed his eyes and raised his hands to the sky. A few seconds later there was movement in the stream. The water, moving slowly at first and then faster, eventually caused the stream to part from one bank to the other, revealing the riverbed. The Prince continued to keep his eyes closed and breathed in heavily. The ground parted and a crack ran through the Earth. A few moments later a gush of warm wind rose from within the Earth. It was very strong and started forcing the water out of the stream, even causing the firmly grounded trees to sway. Out of the earth shot a beam of light, eventually followed by a *crystal*.

A *heart-shaped*, rosewater-coloured crystal floated up on warm air toward the Prince. The wind stopped and the ground closed. Prince Caden opened his eyes and brought his hands to the level of the crystal and let it rest on his left palm. With his other hand, he motioned for the water to flow back into the stream and then for twigs and leaves to rise off the ground and form a case. The Prince uttered some words and the crystal lifted off his palm and hovered above it. A lotus flower began to bloom around the crystal till it wrapped the gem safely within it. With a flick of his hand, Prince Caden manoeuvred the flower to move into the case. He then handed the case to Yayali who hid it close to his heart for protection.

"We should head out," Prince Caden suggested.

They walked back to the village feeling energised and pumped. Prepared to battle and ready to save the World. When they reached the village, the Fae were gathered together, waiting to send them off. Prince Caden turned to them for the last time and said, "This is where we bid you farewell. You will walk through the *Tree of Secrets* and will enter into the *South African* wilderness. The Chief of Magic has created a spell that will transport you to Africa as you walk through the tree. The only thing left to do is for us to pass our blessings on to you."

The five together with Yayali, Quinn and Simha headed in the direction of the Tree of Secrets and the Prince followed. The crowd shared their wishes with the Defenders by throwing flowers at them as they walked toward the tree. They could feel the burst of positive energy showered upon them and they felt the palpable blessings of hope and confidence envelope them. The crowd cheered as they made their way out of Elam.

The Prince walked with them to the entrance of the tree where he handed Yayali a vessel. "I know that you will do us all proud. We believe in you!" he said to the five. He hugged each of them goodbye and he explained once more, "Yayali will protect the stone and he knows what to do with it. When you get to the other side of the tree, you will have to look for *Yana*, the *Tokoloshe,* for he carries the final weapon to unlock the power of the crystal. Good luck!"

As they walked through the tunnel back to the entrance point Samara turned to the others and said, "Is it just me or was this the wrong time for the Prince to drop that on us? I mean who or what the heck is a *Tokoloshe* and where are we supposed to find him?"

"Yes, I agree. That is the sort of thing he could have brought up at breakfast," seconded Nereida with a nod.

"I guess we will figure it out," Viyan comforted.

"We made it this far, what's tracking down one more Guardian?"

They reached the doorway of the tree and stood side by side. One by one they wished each other well before stepping out.

"Good luck team, into the jungle we go," Viyan said.

"Into *battle* we go," Liam corrected.

"It's gonna be wild!" Samara exclaimed as she patted Quinn with her right hand and Simha with her left.

"*Carp diem*, let's seas this moment!" Nerida motivated them.

"That's punny," Samara giggled.

"We got this!" Catori concluded as she looked at her team and nodded.

"Yayali, will you do us the honour?" Viyan asked, gesturing for him to open the door. Yayali stepped up to the bark of the tree. He emptied the contents of the vessel onto the base of the trunk and said, "E sar entered let feer shan (As we entered let us leave)."

The tunnel began to tremble and there were rips of light before the trunk of the tree parted fully, forming a way to the outside.

Chapter Nine

Home

They stepped out from inside the tree and walked into the forest. While the surrounding landscape was green, it was different to the forest that they were in before they had entered Elam. The land was way woodier this time around. There was something different about the air too - different yet familiar. The trees were tall with slender trunks. The forest looked dense from an aerial view, but it was spacious at the base. The trees had some distance between them and the ground was grassy with patches of course, dry, sand.

Viyan led the way through the trees for a bit and then stopped. "Yayali, do you know where to go from here? I do not feel so confident." Viyan felt a strange uncertainty, there was a different presence around them and this altered his sense of instinctual navigation. All of a sudden, there was a rustle of leaves and some of the smaller trees in the vicinity started moving. But there was nothing visible. Again, now much closer to where they stood, the leaves moved as if someone, or something passed by. Still, there was nothing in sight. They were on edge, uncertain of how to react. As they turned to look at each other, Catori felt a sharp wind on her face causing her to back into Viyan. Liam was given a knock on his head by an invisible force. Yayali just smiled and shook his head, not seeming too concerned. He stood still and closed his eyes. Could it be more Fae? African fairies perhaps? *Or was it something else entirely?*

Nereida felt a tap on her shoulder but when she turned to look there was nothing there. They had gotten used to the fairies, as tiny as they could be, the Defenders had become familiar with their appearance. They would be able to spot them. There was clearly something else in the forest with them and this invisible presence was beginning to make them all feel very uneasy. Samara's long loose hair was tossed up in the air and she jumped with a shriek. Yayali, eyes still closed, stuck out his hand as if to grab something. They all turned toward Yayali who seemed to be holding something in his hand, but again, there was nothing visible. Gradually something began to appear. Moments later, an almost mini version of Yayali was dangling from his hand. Yayali held onto a long fur jacket from which hung a human-like creature.

"Please to meet my cousin from far. This is *Tokoloshe*," Yayali introduced the now visible being that he held by his coat.

The creature presented himself with a playful laugh, "I am Fanyana, but call me Yana." He turned to Yayali, "Can you put me down now?"

Yayali looked suspiciously at him. "Only you promise behave."

"Me and promises don't do so well," Yana replied.

Yayali turned to the group who were staring at Yana. "So, you know him then?" Samara asked.

"He does actually bear a resemblance to you," Liam noted.

"And somewhat to you too," Catori said wittily to Liam, reminding him that he too was beast-like, just like them.

Yana straightened his jacket as Yayali placed him back on the ground.

"There were many more of my kind that lived in Elam. It's the centre of magic you know - where all the enchanting creatures lived, together we formed the Fae," he said proudly. "Some of us had chosen to leave Elam and go out into the world so that we could protect the Earth from different corners. I actually have many cousins around the globe. Yayali for one, then there's the Yeti of the Himalayas and the Yowie of Australia," he paused. "Hey! It only struck me just now, seems that one of the criteria is to have a name beginning with a *Y!*"

Yayali interrupted Yana with a big toothy grin, "Everyone say we look same."

Yana was slightly shorter than any of the others. Though he had a boyish build, it was coupled with a noticeably protruding belly. Another common feature that he and Yayali shared, was big feet. While Yana's feet were in shoes, you could tell that they were relatively big for his frame. He also had dark eyes, sharp teeth and distinctive pointy ears that confirmed to the others that he was Fae. In Elam there was no need for Yayali to clothe himself, so he was always *au naturel,* and no one thought anything of it. Yana on the other hand needed to blend in and wore clothing like all the other humans. Because of this it was difficult to tell just how much hair covered his body. But from what was visible, the hair on his head and that which jutted out from the sleeves of his jacket, was dark, thick and of a furry texture. Dressed in human clothing, he could indeed pass for one.

"Oh!" Yana said as he thought of someone else, "Shamus, the legendary leprechaun, used to live in Elam too. He was a bit of a prankster."

"You prankster too," Yayali shouted, pointing a finger at Yana.

Yana was most definitely mischievous but his playfulness was innocent, it was his way of expressing himself and his magic. It was not malicious.

Yana's tone lowered as he explained why he began to play innocent pranks on the villagers. Because they saw him as a threat rather than an aid, he knew that they would never accept him.

"I just wanted to interact with others. I just wanted friends." Yana's eyes began to well as he was reminded how difficult and lonely it was for him. Yayali turned to comfort him. "You still good warrior cousin, now is time come to show it. Time for mission and we here for to get you. We is need you!"

Yana lifted his head to look at Yayali.

He sniffed, smiled and nodded his head before turning to the team to say, "Well what are we waiting for, let's do this!" He began to walk, leading the way.

Samara looked at Catori and Nereida, "Well, that was a quick recovery."

"Yes!" Nereida exclaimed, confused by how quickly Yana's mood had changed.

"And it's nice to meet you too," Catori added.

"Yeah, no need to apologise for that bit of harassment a while ago," Liam added.

Yana heard this and without stopping, turned briefly to look at them.

"I am sorry, old habits die hard," he said as he stomped through the long grass, making a path for the rest to follow. "Sorry for my poor manners. I have been waiting for a long time alone in this forest, so I may be lacking in social etiquette." He turned back to face the path in front of him. "I would venture out from time to time, into the villages and even now into the cities for food and some company. It does get very lonely here, especially coming from a place like Elam which was always so full of energy."

He turned to look at them again, "But I would always come back to the forest, knowing that I had a sacred mission that drew close. I was never gone for long."

"But how did you know that we would be here at this time? How did you know to stay in the forest and this area?" Nereida asked.

"Having left home such a long time ago, my powers are not what they used to be, but I still remember some of my teachings. Years ago when we entered into the forest, I placed an incantation over the space that we had just left. Even though my intuition is not as strong as it initially was, I would get a sense every time there was some sort of movement from the enchanted space. When you arrived, I was immediately drawn back here. There was just a different energy about you. A feeling of home."

"We all do feel a little familiar to each other, I guess," Viyan said as he smiled to the rest of them.

They followed Yana as he made his way through the forest, stomping through the long grass and ferns as they moved between the trees. It was a long walk.

"Is there a place that we could rest? Simha and Quinn need a break and some water," Samara reminded them.

"It is still half a day's trek to Drakensburg so we will need to rest for the night anyway. We will stop in a little while," he replied.

"Trek?" asked Samara.

"Drakensburg?" Nereida questioned.

"He means a journey," Viyan explained to Samara. He then turned to Nereida, "Drakensburg is the highest mountain range in Southern Africa. It extends into Lesotho, and forms part of the Great Escarpment," he verbalised, as if reading a dictionary definition.

Viyan paused and then turned to Yana to ask, "But why are we going there? Is this where we need to be - where the mission is?"

"No. We have to make one more stop before we can get to the mission's location. We have to meet one more Guardian on the way." He turned around to look directly at them all before saying, "And your transportation to that location is with him."

"Finally, no more walking!" Nereida exclaimed.

"I hope it has aircon," Samara said, wiping the sweat from her brow.

"You could say that it's … somewhat of a drop-top," Yana replied. Having lived among the humans for many changing years, Yana had picked up on their languages and ways of life. He had assimilated authentically into the human way.

They followed Yana a short distance to a stream where they stopped for a break. "We can rest here on the banks of this stream for the night. It is safe and we will have some drinking water too."

As Yana spoke, Simha headed to the stream to drink. The water flowed down the mountains of the Drakensburg, which were now nearby. The sun had almost set so Yana began to light a fire. They heated the food which they had brought with them from Elam and shared the meal while Quinn grazed on the leaves. As Yana tasted the food, bouts of happiness engulfed him. "I can taste home," he expressed warmly, in complete contentment.

"I have been here in Africa for a very, very long time now but I can still remember how different the food was, and exactly what it tasted like."

Satisfied, he rubbed his belly. He began to share his story as he continued to nibble on the food. "I left Elam with some of my cousins – other fairies and goblins. We were a strong team of warriors who entered into the African forest as we made our way through the Tree of Secrets. We knew the way of Elam but the outer world was a different experience for us. It took some time to find ourselves out here. This was many, many moons ago and there were only a few villages around at the time. We searched till we finally came across people."

He thought back to his first experience meeting humans. "We were so excited! We tried to befriend the villagers, but they were afraid of us. We meant no harm, we just wanted to connect with others. But we looked strange and unfamiliar to them." He looked at his hands. "I don't blame them. They were frightened to see others that didn't look like them. I guess I would be scared to."

In an effort to comfort him, Liam placed a hand on Yana's shoulder. He smiled at Liam and then continued his tale. "We got the same treatment from one village to the next and by the time we had reached the third village, they had already heard of us and were prepared for our arrival. The villagers were told that we were dangerous and so they were prepared to kill us. Many of the family that I came with were terrified and returned to Elam or other lands." He stopped briefly. "Well, I hope that they returned, I never heard from some of them after. A few of us carried on journeying to other villages, hopeful that we could find permanent shelter. Sadly, we kept getting rejected and threatened. Eventually, there was only me. Because of my powers of invisibility and space jumping, I could live undetected for some time in the villages. I used to try to even help them, but because of their fear, they mistook my helpfulness for harmfulness."

Yana's story was heartful as he explained how he tried to help the villagers that he had encountered. You could understand from his tone that he wanted nothing more than company, and it was evident that he was rather lonely.

"They created stories about me, depicting me as evil and vengeful and said that I was using dark magic. These stories described me as everything that I was not. They didn't realise that I was only trying to help, they still just saw me as a threat." Yana paused to take a nibble of food.

"Back then people were not aware of the possible dangers of indoor fires and would sleep in small rooms with burning flames. Many lost their lives this way. I would try to warn them about sleeping too close to the fire, but this just became a tale of how I would attack sleeping victims and take their lives. To prevent any of my *attacks*, people started sleeping on raised beds." He paused to think.

"On the positive side, it probably did save a few lives."

He mulled over the thought. He had not realised it, but he had accomplished something good in his time in Africa. All these years he assumed that he was worthless when in fact he had made a difference. He felt proud of himself.

"I did not know how long I would need to stay here for. Honestly, I did not know if I ever would be returning home. What I did know though, was that I couldn't hide forever and for as long as I would be in Africa, among humans, I would need to find a way to live with them. Eventually, to blend in, I adopted their ways. I dressed and spoke like them and for the first time, they accepted me! If I think back to the first interactions, they definitely were surprised by my appearance. I'm pretty sure that they thought I had a disfigurement but did not want to be inconsiderate to ask any questions. They did stare though, especially the kids. But now I am just one of the townsfolk and that's all there is to it.

"Share a few details about those pranks," Liam enquired, interested in gathering some arsenal for his box of tricks. The air was filled with laughter as Yana told them of some of the jokes that he would play on the villagers. Innocent little trickeries, like moving furniture around or hiding people's belongings. And a few more impactful stunts like embarrassing the village bullies in public. He knew his limitations though and would never harm anyone. But being by oneself for a very, very long time, was lonely and he needed to find ways to entertain himself. Perhaps it was the effects of being alone for so long, but he had a very innocent child-like nature about him. He was playful and it was evident that being so brought him joy.

As Samara listened to his stories, she thought about how he would have been such a successful comedian. *What different lives some people could have lived, if only they had belonged to a different world.* It made her reflect on how big the Earth really was, and how many different people lived on it. How many were living in their own worlds, assuming that it was the only existence? And at that very minute, not a single one of those lives was aware of what was transpiring.

So many naïve souls, so many unknowing lives to save, she thought.

Yana possessed a unique storytelling quality and kept them entertained for most of the evening. Before going to sleep, they discussed the plans for the next day's journey and then divided the night watch into shifts so that they all could rest.

The next morning, they were awoken by the bright sun as it rose from behind the mountains. Freshening up with the crisp water from the Tugela River, they felt revived. It was pure and refreshing, too cold to bathe in but cool enough to drink. Once Catori cleansed the water through an invocation, it was safe for them to consume.

"Perhaps we can start the journey and gather some food on the way," Yana suggested. "There are some orchards along the path and if we don't waste time, we can reach our destination around midday."

He led the way along the bank of the stream, and they followed, trying to stay focused on the path.

A few kilometres into the journey, Catori noticed that the forest to the left of them, opposite of the river, was beginning to become sparse.

"It seems that we are nearing the end of the forest. It should be only grasslands ahead," she said.

They passed the last trees of the forest and entered the open fields where the grass and ferns continued to grow on the ground. The mountains were now clearly visible in the near distance. The river had narrowed into a stream and had become shallower, revealing rocks at the stream's boundary. The river's source could be recognised. They had reached the Tugela Gorge. As they stopped, deciding where to go, they noticed someone in the distance, on the opposite end of the stream, walking toward them. He had come from the direction of the nearby town. The man wore a black hooded mid-length trench coat.

"Ramiel!" Yana shouted out as the man neared them.

How did Yana know this person? Was he a friend? Surely, he could not be one of them, not the person they were there to find? He looked so, so ordinary!

"Ramiel, it has been so long my brother!" Yana said as he went up to hug the man. He lowered the hood from over his head and they could see him clearly. Yana turned to the others to introduce the stranger, "Meet Ramiel, the last of the Guardians to gather."

Ramiel looked at them and smiled. "I am pleased to finally meet you all." His words were clear and spoken in a deep, husky tone. Perhaps it was his tone that mirrored his appearance. He was tall and big – not fat but muscular - had shoulder-length wavy, dark hair and his skin was an olive to tan complexion. He was very attractive and looked as if he could have been in his early thirties.

"What's up with the coat dress code? It's like a bijillion degrees out here," Samara whispered to Catori.

"You all must be hungry," Ramiel said, looking at them.

Was he reading their minds? Apart from greeting them, that was a rather unusual first point of conversation.

"I will take you to get something to eat. It is not too far from here. But we need to hurry, the time is drawing near so we need to make haste."

He led them to an orchard a little way off the path that they were walking on, away from the gorge. At the sight of the fruit, they ran into the field and began to pluck them off the tree without hesitation. There were rows of different fruit trees; apples, pears, and figs, and to the side were rows and rows of strawberry bushes growing close to the ground. The fruit looked ripe and juicy and Samara and Nereida tore into the strawberries as they pulled them from the vines.

"Oh my! How absolutely delicious!" Nereida exclaimed as she bit into the fruit.

"Take as much as you can but we need to hurry before anyone sees us, these orchards are not for outsiders," Ramiel warned.

They plucked the fruit off the various trees and placed them into the satchels that they had carried the food in.

For every strawberry that Samara stored, she ate one. She stopped for a second between berries to sweep the hair away from her face, and as she did, she caught a glimpse of the mountains in full view behind the orchard. She stared in wonder. The range painted a picturesque backdrop to the orchards. With the mountains in the background and the sun peering through the fluffy white clouds, the trees of the orchards with the plump, ripe fruit created pops of colour across the fresh, green grasslands.

"*Gorgeous!*" Samara uttered in a daze.

"All right, we need to get a move on!" Ramiel yelled as he interrupted her moment of wonderment. "We will take the gatherings to a spot where we can eat and rest. I will leave you there at the foot of the mountain while I fetch my companion. We will then go to the destination together. But for now, follow me." Ramiel had the plan already figured out.

They left the orchards and walked toward the mountains again. It had become somewhat overcast and heavy clouds began to form. The mountains were now closer, but their peaks were covered in light grey skies. The sun was clouded over, making the walk a bit gloomy. As they made their way toward the range, the air above their heads was dense due to the low-hanging clouds. Reaching the base of the mountain, Ramiel stopped. "We should rest here for a while and eat," he said, gesturing to a spot.

Although slightly rocky the soft green grass provided a comfortable resting space. The sun was now shining down on them through the clouds as they sat on the grass to enjoy the fruit they had gathered. Viyan turned to Ramiel to ask, "So we know how Yana came to Africa, is your story the same?"

"Maybe at the beginning," he confirmed.

"I left Elam many years before Yana did. Everyone in Elam knew about *The Threat* and what our role as Guardians would be to stop it. I was one of the first to leave and venture out into the greater world, even before the changes to the Earth began. When I left Elam, I left with a dragon's egg."

"*Khaleesi!*" Samara exclaimed.

"I think you mean *Father of Dragons*," Liam indicated. Samara agreed.

Ramiel gave them a look as if to let them know that they were being rude.

"Please continue, *Khal*," Samara offered with a hand gesture.

Ramiel ignored her and finished the story. "There was a time when dragons roamed freely in the world but like so many other creatures, they eventually died out. We could not prevent this extinction as it was their fate, but we did try to rescue the last dragon and take her with us to Elam where we thought we could help her. Sadly, she had been injured and could not be saved in time. But she had carried with her a baby, the very last dragon egg in existence. She was destined to be part of our mission. I brought her with me when I left Elam and have been guarding her ever since. It has been my duty up until now to protect her, she is like my little sister. My daughter even," Ramiel said with a lump in his throat.

"When that egg hatched, she had not only become one of the most magnificent creatures ever but also one of the rarest. No one in the outer world knows of her existence except for Yana and I, and now you. And soon you will have the honour of meeting *Baby*," Ramiel crowed, as a truly proud father would.

"So have you been hiding all this time, just protecting her?" Viyan asked. "Was it not safer to stay in Elam with her?"

"Oh no, not hidden!" Ramiel exclaimed. "We have been here a long, long, time. Dragon eggs take a while to hatch. When we arrived it was very safe, and you have to remember that dragons once roamed freely on Earth. I have been here when all there was were mountains and forests. When the villages and then towns developed, I just adapted and settled with the changes. The town is about 8 kilometres away, not far from the orchards that we were in."

"Well, you look like any other human, so I imagine that you fitted in comfortably," Liam confirmed.

"It took some adjusting to get used to the humans and their ways but yes I look just like them, so it was not difficult to pretend to be one," Ramiel agreed. "But the town became too overpopulated and a tourist hub. That became a risk for Baby. Also, everything became so commercial and unnatural with reproduced foods."

"*Do you mean fast food?*" Samara asked.

"Yes, that is what it's called."

"You mean to say that there has been food, like actual, nourishing, tasty food, just a few miles away from us?" Samara moaned.

"But you just ate!" Viyan exclaimed.

"It's not the same! This is natural and healthy, and I will be hungry in five minutes again. I need something more sustainable," she contested.

"I am going to leave you here for a while to finish your food before we head off to our final destination," Ramiel affirmed, as he turned to look at the mountain. "You can wait here at the base while I head up. I shouldn't be too long. Rest in that time and gather up your strength. You are going to need it!"

As they watched Ramiel get ready to leave, they assumed that he was going to walk up the mountain and wondered how long a hike to the peak would take.

"Are you sure it won't be long? It seems like it is going to be a very long climb," Samara indicated as she looked up to survey the height of the mountain.

"It is! But luckily I don't have to walk!" Ramiel gloated.

The clouds had now disappeared completely and gave way to the sun, revealing the very top of the mountain which Ramiel needed to reach. It was a great ascent to the peak, and it looked very rocky. Despite all that sunshine, it seemed that it would be extremely cold at the top. This is why they were baffled when Ramiel took off the trench that he was wearing to stand in a sleeveless t-shirt. Ramiel rolled his shoulders back and moved his head from side to side to stretch his neck. Unexpectedly, from behind him, wings began to expand. Wings that were clearly not there when he took his coat off. They were magnificent – soft-grey, angelic, marvellous wings! The group gasped in surprise. None of them had expected that to happen!

"Well that's not something you see every day now," Liam commented.

"You're a werewolf! How are you the surprised one?" Viyan retorted.

"Touché!" Liam exclaimed as he nodded his head, both of them just gawking at Ramiel.

"Were they hidden?" Nereida asked hesitantly. "Because we did not see anything at the back of you."

"They are in fact always there; they are just invisible. I can make them appear when I need them. When I was in Elam, I always had them visible, but when I came here I had to hide them, for obvious reasons."

He looked up at the mountain.

"I only use them when I need to go up to see Baby."

As he said that, he began to flap his wings. "I will fly up there quickly to get him."

Viyan stared thoughtfully at the mountain range, "So I guess that's why they call them *Dragon Mountains*."

Ramiel began to levitate off the ground before taking off at lightning speed, leaving behind a gush of wind. The view of Ramiel flying up the mountain and toward the blazing sun in front of him reminded Samara of Icarus. *"Not too close to the sun!"* she warned, as he flew up.

Once he left, the rest ran at Yana bombarding him with questions about Ramiel.

"What about the dragon?" Liam asked.

"Yes, have you heard about her? Have you seen her?" Samara interjected.

"Were you around when the dragon hatched?" Catori asked.

"Is she temperamental? Like a Kraken?" Nereida chirped, excited to know.

Yana smiled and put a hand up, gesturing to stop the questions.

After all his family had returned to Elam, he was lost and alone. Despite his mission, he felt like he could not continue through the loneliness. Ramiel was drawn to Yana's aching heart and found him. He lived a few years with Ramiel and helped him raise the baby dragon. They nursed her and trained her. They taught Baby how and when to feed so that she would not be spotted. "She goes out only in the early hours of the morning before the break of dawn or when it is still very dark. She feeds on the fruit of the high trees as well as on birds and smaller animals and twice a week hunts for game and larger animals. Baby was easier to train when she was little but now that she is bigger, she knows how to be … what is the word?" Yana paused. "*Stealth*!" he exclaimed.

"He has learnt to hunt creatures in the distant open grasslands, and he flies off to far-away farms to hunt, not from the neighbouring ones."

"Why did you return to live on your own after reuniting with someone from your home? Was it not better and less lonely if you all stayed together?" Nereida asked, feeling sad for Yana.

"As the villages became modernised towns, it became more dangerous for us. We realised that if we lived as individuals, we could be less visible and so we decided to split up to protect Baby. It was a difficult choice, but we knew that it was for the best. We thought that it would be better to blend in than try to hide away. It was much easier for Ramiel to do. I am always in this coat and glasses to cover up."

He turned to look at Liam, "Oh, how much simpler my life would have been if I had your powers."

Liam was taken by Yana's words. He had never thought of his lycanthropy as a power, it was just something he always knew. A curse mostly, but not a power. It was a part of him - a responsibility. But Yana was right, it really was an advantage, because out in the bigger world, this difference was his power. He had a newfound appreciation for who he was. How had he been so blind to his gift all this time?

The group was seated on the grass, enjoying the beautiful landscape when Catori spotted something in the distance. It was flying fast toward them, and it was gigantic. It made its way directly to them but then flew over. They felt a gush of strong wind and stood up instinctively. The gigantic creature had flown overhead and then came in from behind them. As the creature got closer, their hair and clothes blew in the wind before they themselves were almost fully tossed aside. The beast landed with a loud THUD, and retracted its wings when it did. They stood in awe at its size. Ramiel flew in, landing next to the monster. He caught his breath before introducing it.

"This is *Baby*, my little dragon," he said as he rubbed the beast.

"Little?" Catori remarked sarcastically.

"Baby?" Samara asked.

"Ok, so I am not so creative with the names. But she is just that, my little baby."

The creature had the physique and appearance of a Komodo dragon, but its body was not low to the ground. It had longish, tree stump looking legs and a long thick tail that was pointed at the tip. It also had a fork-like tongue and thick armoured skin.

"Yeah, she is really, um, cute!" Samara said as she sized her up.

"I sure hope she doesn't bite!" Nereida added fearfully.

As she said this, Simha made his way to stand in front of the dragon.

"No Simha, come here boy!" Samara yelled as she tried to call him back, fearing that the dragon would eat him whole.

Viyan held her hand to stop her. "No, it's ok!"

There was silence as everyone watched the two creatures, waiting to see the outcome of their interaction. The dragon bowed her head in a respectful gesture to Simha and Simha barked in acknowledgement.

"She likes you all!" Ramiel celebrated as he brushed his hand over Baby.

"Ok, we need to plan our next move," Ramiel said gathering everyone up.

They all moved in closer.

"Do you know where the exact location is?" Catori asked Ramiel.

"We need to head to the coast of Accra in Ghana. That is where the centre of the Earth is."

"Sorry, did you say *Centre of the Earth*?" Samara confirmed.

"Yes."

"So, the centre of the Earth is an actual point, not a Vernian story plot?" Viyan clarified.

"Jules Verne actually based a lot of his writing on possible truths, that's why he has such a great following till today," Liam confirmed.

Viyan began to look around and felt uneasy. He paced a little. "Does anyone else feel slightly strange? Maybe I ate too much or had some bad fruit?" he asked, trying to figure out the cause of the unsettling feeling. Quinn neighed and shook his head as he stomped his foot on the ground.

"It is not just you," Yana said as he comforted Quinn.

"The Earth is very weak and the protective ozone can no longer hold. The Negative Energies are entering Earth and it's causing this misplace of energetic feel," Ramiel said, confirming what the change in mood was. "We have to go now! We have to restore the balance before it's too late," he added.

"Ok! So how exactly do we do this?" Liam asked, trying to work out the logistics.

"I have thought about it, and this will be the best option. Viyan, Catori, Nereida, Liam, Yayali and Simha will ride on Baby and I will fly beside her. Yana and I have been there before so he knows where to go. He can teleport there," Ramiel explained as he directed everyone on what to do.

"I think I will be able to take Simha with me," Yana aided. "After all, he does have a little magic in him too." He winked at the dog. "But I am going to need some help from Simha. Yayali, you are not going to fit comfortably on Baby so you are going to have to come with us too."

"Ok, cool, cool, cool," Samara said shaking her head as she followed the plans. "So, Quinn and I will just hang around here and wait for you guys to come back and get us then?"

"Oh, I assumed that you knew how you would get there since you have Quinn after all," Ramiel replied. "You two will fly beside me."

"You mean that the two of us fly alone?" Samara asked confused.

"Quinn is fly. He is very good to flying," Yayali said as he smiled at Quinn while petting his mane.

Just then Quinn, as Ramiel had done, revealed a magnificent pair of hidden wings. They were a captivating, iridescent shade of pearl.

"Quinn! You mean I didn't have to walk all along, you could have been flying me around this whole time?! Of all the things to hide from me!" Samara laughed excitedly, surprised by the discovery.

"I hope that we will all fit!" Nereida exclaimed as she tried to climb onto the dragon.

"It may be a squeeze but he is a fast flier, so it won't be too long," Ramiel said. "Yana, I think you go first so that we know if you three can make it over."

"You are right!" Yana agreed with Ramiel.

The three, Yana, Yayali and Simha, stood in a huddle.

"Ready Simha?" Yana asked.

He then hugged onto Simha and Yayali before closing his eyes tight to concentrate. In the blink of an eye, they vanished.

"Right! It's our turn now," Ramiel said as he turned around to face the rest of them. They had all boarded the dragon and were getting ready for take-off when Yana reappeared.

"We made it, we are at the coast. But hurry, they are many already and we cannot fight them off."

Ramiel nodded in agreement and then Yana vanished again.

"We need to hurry!" Ramiel looked at Baby and then Quinn and nodded to them both. Quinn began to flap his wings and took off instantly. Baby extended her wings creating a massive wingspan. She slowly flapped her wings and then increased the speed to create a surge of wind before taking off. Ramiel followed them both. Despite its mass, the dragon was an extremely fast flier.

"Woohoo!" Samara shouted in the air as she held onto Quinn's neck. The others held on tightly to the speeding dragon for fear of falling.

"It really is beautiful up here," Catori said.

"I wouldn't know!" Liam said with his eyes shut tight.

They flew over the mountains at an incredible speed. It was uncomfortably high and very cold. Liam felt his back to make sure that his spear was still attached. He really was not enjoying the ride. Quinn, Baby and Ramiel flew separately for a bit before they all managed to reach the same speed. They needed to maintain some stability in the air before they could come together. Baby and Quinn were flying side by side when

Ramiel flew in between the two of them. With his right hand he held onto Quinn around his withers and with his left arm he gripped Baby.

"Hold on tight!" Ramiel warned.

"What?" Liam asked, unable to hear.

"I said. Hold. On. Tight!" Ramiel shouted.

But before Liam could ask him a second time what he had said, they were flying at a lightning-fast speed. Ramiel was what folklore called the *Impundula*, The *Lightning Bird* of Africa. While the African stories told of a wicked creature, Ramiel was anything but. Apart from being able to fly at extraordinary speed, he also had the power to summon lightning.

They flew at such incredible speed that it looked as if they were being teleported – it seemed as though their bodies were not whole but fragmented. They could not make complete sense of what was happening, but to them it seemed as if they were still and everything around them was just a blur. The whole journey took mere minutes and then their speed slowly reduced. As if at first they were catapulted and now were slowing down. The grounds below were becoming visible. There was greenery and mountain ranges and, in the distance, they could see the ocean.

"Does anyone else feel like their stomach is in their mouth?" Liam asked.

"At least you can tell which of your organs is which!" Viyan responded.

They slowly began to descend to the grounds below. The landing point was supposed to be an open, uninhabited land, but it was clear that there were people below and they were not ordinary citizens. They all wore the same clothes, the same uniform. This was an army!

The Defenders flew closer to the Earth, preparing to land. The group fighting below noticed Baby's arrival and due to the wind force from Baby's wings they began to disperse as she neared the ground. Ramiel landed on the earth first where he stood with his wings expanded. Baby landed next to him with a heavy drop onto the sand, causing a cloud of dust. Viyan, Catori, Liam and Nereida took a few moments to catch their bearings before each climbed off Baby and onto the ground. Quinn then landed with Samara and she immediately jumped off to join the others. Ramiel retracted his wings and stood beside them, side-by-side, in a defensive battle pose. He looked into the distance and could see Yayali and Yana fighting off the enemy. Finally, after all the journeying, meeting and gathering of the Guardians, they were at their point of purpose. They instinctively drew their weapons, preparing to help their friends as they charged toward the army.

The Defenders had ensured the safety of their weapons the entire journey, waiting for this very moment to use them. Viyan pulled out the *trident*, Samara drew her *sword*, Catori revealed her *bow and arrow* and Liam his *spear*. Nereida removed the *conch* from the satchel that she carried across her body. They were ready for battle!

Chapter Ten

The Battle

The sky above the land upon which Yayali and Yana fought looked as if it had been split apart, as though the heavens had been ripped. Beams of light fell rapidly from this tear in the sky and as they reached the ground, they took on a human avatar. These Energies fell to Earth as if they were drawn to it like a magnet. They were few at first but as the portal in the sky widened, they created a scene of hundreds of light pillars shooting down. While these forms may have looked human, they were not. They were pure energy. Energy forms that needed a planet to live on; a new home since theirs was destroyed, and they needed to take on an earthly body when they entered the Earth's atmosphere. While the aliens that entered the oceans did so as animals to battle in water, these chose a human appearance. Under Rahu's instruction, they would need to fight Man if they wanted to inhabit Earth, so assuming the same form would allow them to mimic humans.

As the Guardians had learnt, these Energies came from other planets which were consumed by negative energy and eventually destroyed because of it. Since Earth had immense and varying life and so much resultant energy, mostly positive, it could provide a home for these life forces to survive in.

They needed positive energy as a source because it provided sustenance for life. They were not trying to take over the World, they were just looking for a home. The problem was that these negative forces, by their nature, would eventually consume and then convert all the positive energy into negative energy. This would eventually destroy Earth. *The Battle* that the Guardians were destined to fight was to save Earth from this destruction.

The group had landed close to the Atlantic Ocean and could make sight of the shore. As the Defenders neared, they saw Yayali wielding his club and Yana hurling his discus at these newly formed humanoids. Yana's weapon was the *discus*; a flat metal disc with a serrated edge and a hollow centre which radiated a force of kinetic energy controlled through Yana's will. All this time he had hidden it under the coat that he always wore.

As the humanoids were destroyed, they retracted in reverse from the way that they were formed. Their human form instantly disappeared leaving a small trail of dust as their energy was absorbed back through the portal.

The portal continuously opened, allowing more Energies in. The rest of the Defenders joined to help Yana and Yayali as the creatures fell to Earth in increasing numbers. The six charged toward their team, fighting off the humanoids in their path. Samara swung her sword while Catori drew her bow, firing off arrows at the enemy as they ran toward Yana and Yayali. The Energies were sucked back into the sky, leaving dust clouds behind. As Viyan, Liam, Samara, Nereida, Catori and Ramiel reached the three, they formed a barricade to help them fight off the growing enemy.

Together they moved forward to attack, but it was useless. There were just too many. The Defenders stood with their backs toward each other as they retreated into a group.

"These beings are coming in very fast," Catori shouted. "I don't know how much longer we will be able to fight them off if they keep increasing in numbers."

"Our only chance is to get the portal to stop opening," Liam added before tossing his spear at the growing crowd.

"Or to close altogether!" Nereida suggested. "Under the sea, the portals would close after some time, they never remained open, and then they would disappear forever," she advised.

"But this one is different. This is the main portal," Ramiel explained. "The negative energy over time has weakened the ozone but it is the dark energy from Rahu that keeps the portal open. Only when we destroy him, can we finally close the portal. This is what we must do. This is the mission; to eliminate these Energies and to close the portal."

Viyan realised that there was another way to do this – it came to him in thought. "Yes, this is our mission, but it does not have to be done in this order. We need to close the portal first and this will stop the Energies from entering."

"That's logical! But how do you propose we do that? How can we reverse in a few minutes what has been happening over millennia?" Ramiel asked.

"I know how, and it is why we are all here together!" Viyan exclaimed.

"Well, you better tell us quickly because we are losing this battle as humans. We need a different approach!" Liam yelled as he tossed his spear at the enemy once again. Liam's spear was connected to him through his DNA. Like a boomerang it would make its way back to him after being thrown. "You take over, use my spear!" he told Ramiel. As he ran forward, he morphed into his werewolf counterpart. It was an instant transformation. He ran, rapidly increasing his speed until he leapt toward the enemy. In mid-air he took on his alternate form as his body contorted from human to wolf.

Ramiel threw the spear at the aliens but he could not control it the same as Liam. He would need to use it as a traditional weapon. Samara turned to look at Ramiel next to her. *Just a pretty face*, she thought to herself. Apart for those magnificent wings, it did not seem like Ramiel had much else to offer in the fight. Liam picked up the spear in his mouth and dropped it at Ramiel's feet before sprinting off again to fight.

Viyan instinctively took control of the situation. "Nereida, we are going to need help from the ocean on this. Do you think you could summon some of the creatures from below?"

Nereida nodded in agreement. She held onto her conch and brought it to her lips as she began to run toward the ocean. She blew into it and it emitted a sonic blast, destroying the Energies in front of her and clearing a path toward the ocean. While she managed to get a little closer to the shore, she was still a distance from the water. She stopped running and stood still on the sand. Nereida concentrated on the space slightly above her eyes as she tried to sense life within the ocean. Using a similar method to dolphins and whales, she was trying to echolocate and communicate with nearby ocean life. Her focused concentration reached into the ocean where she was able to make contact with creatures swimming toward the shore. It was her underwater defence army. The Sirens were already on their way to help them in the battle. With a sense of relief, Nereida returned to the Defenders.

"We have to move closer to the shore," she said. "Eimear and the others are coming."

"Yayali!" Viyan shouted. "We are going to need Yantra soon. Hold onto it securely."

Yayali double-tapped his chest to indicate that it was safe.

"We have to move closer toward the ocean," Viyan shouted to the others.

At the sight of the falling Energies, Samara thought of ways to escape the army and move toward the shore. She instantly devised strategies within her mind. She analysed them all, selecting and declining the options. She knew which plan to execute. Instinctively she assumed her full warrior mode and the defender in her fearlessly came to the surface.

"You go and I will defend from the back," she called to the others.

"*No!*" instructed Viyan. "You can't protect us alone!"

"Yes, I can. I have been training for this for centuries. Trust me, I know what I have to do. I will be behind you and will follow you directly to the shore."

Catori and Nereida looked worryingly at Samara. How could she be the one making this sacrifice? Surely it had to be one of them, someone who had intentionally been preparing for this fight, to defend the rest. Liam had trained for this, he knew how to defend the pack from behind, he should do it, or at least stay with her. But for some reason, no one said anything. As if this was what Samara alone was meant to do.

"She can do this!" Ramiel supported, interrupting the silence.

Samara looked at Viyan and assured him. "I can do this," she said softly as she looked into his eyes.

"Let us not waste any more time," Ramiel shouted as he started making his way toward the shore.

Viyan was reluctant but he agreed to let her be the warrior she was meant to be.

The Defenders maintained a line formation as they fought off the Energies, with Liam leading the pack as his wolf metamorph. As they moved toward the shore, the land became grassier and it began to slope slightly as they moved from atop a mountainous range to a lower-lying terrain at the coastline. Samara fought off the Energies as she swung her sword while Quinn and Simha remained by her side helping. She looked ahead as the Defenders made their way toward the shore. Although she was supposed to be right behind them, as she had agreed, she had instead planned to stay and create a distraction. This was the approach that she had selected. Samara tried hard to fight them off, instinctively recalling the training that she had learnt as a samurai and a warrior. But as the humanoids increasingly fell onto Earth, they formed faster than Samara could manage. Eventually, the three were trapped in a circle formed by the aliens, separating them from the other Defenders.

As the humanoids charged toward the three, Samara knew that there was no way that she could fight them all. In her mind she called for Durga, asking for help, but nothing happened. Samara closed her eyes knowing that the end was near but more so that she had failed. As she considered all the other strategies that she should have used instead, she realised that she had applied the only one that would have worked. The only option that would have allowed the Defenders to get to the shore.

Why was her purpose so short-lived? Awakening to a calling that lasted for such a short time – what was the point? As she questioned, she felt a charge grow inside. She knew that her mission could not end there, she was not ready for it to. She was supposed to fulfil her destiny and save the Earth, side by side with the other Guardians. It was her purpose, her calling. *She was not ready to die!*

She braced for impact from the swarming Energies, but instead of the anticipated pain, she felt a warmth. Comforting and bright like the sun. She immediately believed in herself, believed that she was one of the chosen ones for a reason. That the prophecy was precise, and that she WOULD save the World. But even deeper, she felt a sense of empowerment in knowing that this was what she was meant to do. That her whole life was leading up to this very moment and that she was not a failure. She was just waiting for her time.

When she opened her eyes, Quinn was emitting an energy field that shielded them from the enemy. They were encased within a protective field of light that the humanoids were unable to enter. Within this light field, beside Samara, she witnessed her companion Simha grow in size. He transformed from a tame Chow-Chow to a ferocious lion. All of this happened as if time had slowed down within the light field, allowing for this transformation. *As if someone was intervening.* Simha let out a vicious roar and Samara regained her focus. Without wasting any more time, she instinctively mounted Quinn and began to charge toward the shore. She drew her sword to defend them against the enemy as they rode off. But this time Simha no longer needed any defending and he tore through the Energies as they made their way toward the shore.

The rest of the Defenders had found their way down the slope to where the grassy land turned into sandy beach. Almost at the shore, catching their breath, Viyan and the others turned around to look for Samara, growing anxious with worry. They waited in anticipation with their eyes glued to the top of the slope. Viyan's mind raced, regretting leaving Samara behind. *I should have known better. How could I leave my little sister? I should have been the one to stay. Why did I not offer to be the one? She is too young! Why did I not at least stay with her? I should have said something!*

Viyan was about to head back when on the peak of the incline they saw her. Samara had made her way to the top of the hill where she stopped, looking down at the rest of them. She jumped off Quinn to stand beside Simha. And as she placed her hand on his head, the sun beaming on them both, she looked poetic. The Defenders stared at her in wonder. In that very imagery, with her long, wavy hair flowing in the breeze, the light bouncing off her, and Simha by her side, she resembled the Durga that Viyan saw in his dreams. She embodied the *Goddess*. She had become the *warrior* that she had trained to be. She was … *The Defender.*

Samara waved at the others, gesturing for them to move closer to the shore while she made her way down to the base. Samara, Simha and Quinn headed straight for the shoreline. Close behind them, the enemy was fast approaching. Samara caught up to the other Defenders who were now standing side by side facing the ocean. With a heavy breath, she asked as she joined them, "So what do we do now?"

"So far we just needed to get here, I do hope that we have a plan now that we are here," Yana said in a slight panic.

Liam, now in his human form, began to pace anxiously back and forth on the beach. "There's nowhere to go from here. Once they reach us, that's it!" he panicked.

Viyan pointed at the ocean while explaining to them what the plan was.

"A few miles into the ocean is a location called 'Null Island'. It is a small invisible island that is precisely above the centre of the Earth. We need to get the sacred gem to Null Island. That rose-quartz stone is the heart source that we need to use to help re-energise the Earth. Yantra has been protected all these years because it is the only thing that can restore the core, or rather the heart of the Earth." Viyan took a breath before explaining further, "But the stone can only be activated by us. Each one of you Guardians holds the power within your weapons as well as within yourselves. And it will take our combined power to charge the stone. Yantra is exceptionally powerful and to prevent its misuse if it was ever stolen, it could not be triggered without all of us selected Guardians present."

Viyan looked at them with bright, sparkling eyes. He believed in them and in the mission and felt confident in himself. He found his path again. In true leader form, he raised the triton, "This is what you were born for! Your time is finally here!" he bellowed.

The others raised their weapons and cheered in motivation.

Viyan walked over to Samara and hugged her, "I knew you could do it! I don't know how you managed to, but you did. *I am so proud of you!*"

He looked into her eyes, "This is your purpose, and we WILL win."

As the words of encouragement left his lips, a dark shadow eclipsed the sun. They watched as it passed over, glooming the surrounding.

"*Rahu is here!*" Ramiel said despairingly as each one felt a chill course through them.

The enemy had now made it onto the beach and their numbers had grown once again. More and more were making their way onto Earth as the portal continued to widen. Baby had flown up to the sky to try to fight off as many as she could but her efforts were thwarted. As she saw them getting closer, Catori closed her eyes and focused on the sky. She used the force of nature to summon the wind. A gush of air blew in and created a fierce sandstorm to distract the enemy and create a barrier between them and the Defenders. As the sandstorm grew it blocked visibility for both the Defenders and the aliens. Catori managed to keep the storm in position to buy the Defenders some time.

"How do we get the stone to Null Island?" Liam asked Viyan.

Viyan was distracted, as though he was visualising something. *Was he devising a strategy or was he foreseeing an event?*

"V!" Samara yelled.

Viyan looked at her as she broke him from his trance.

"We need you! Now!" she shouted.

"Right!" Viyan responded, as he came to. "Nereida, are the Sirens close to the shore?"

"Yes, they are in the water, close by where we stand," she confirmed.

"We are going to have to get Yantra to Eimear to transport it to Null Island…"

Before Viyan could expound the strategy, the enemy broke through the storm. The sand was vicious, stinging as it flew in a torrent. Still, they pushed through and were heading for the Defenders. Catori could no longer hold the storm and let it subside.

The humanoids were now free and began to charge toward the Defenders. Baby, unable to fight the Energies close to the portal, returned to the shore and to the others. Just as the enemy was almost at the Defenders, Baby landed on the ground next to Ramiel. Ramiel flew onto the dragon's back.

"Now Baby!" he howled.

She extended her neck forward, opened her mouth and spat out a furnace. The dragon walked forward, continuously blowing out flames, destroying the humanoids. The endless stream of fire did not even allow for any traces of dust to be witnessed after the Energies retraction. The fire lessened before Baby sucked back the last few flames.

"Good job girl!" Ramiel praised, as he rubbed the dragon's head.

Baby had managed to destroy the humanoids close to the shore but the active portal meant that more would soon follow and that they would eventually outnumber and destroy the Guardians on land, and in the water, if something was not done immediately to stop them from entering Earth's atmosphere. If the Guardians were unable to seize control now, they would not be able to win the battle.

The Defenders were unaware but Baby's fiasco of fire had created a distraction. As Baby fought off the humanoids, an enormous snake crawled out from the trees and made its way onto the beach. No one had seen this creature prior to that moment. Its appearance was sudden and terrifying as it began to travel with increasing speed directly toward the Defenders. *Was this Rahu?*

Samara thought that this could very well be the evil that the Chief warned them of; the leader that they were missioned to destroy. Everyone knows that a snake is hardly ever associated with good.

They stood frozen at the sight of the snake, unsure of what to do because they hadn't planned for this interception. Without a word to each other, thoughts began to flow into each Defender's mind, prompting them to intuitively act. Nereida aimed her conch at the ocean and blew into it. This caused the sea to create intense waves. The snake made its way directly toward Yayali and as it neared him, it grew steadily in size. Yayali, witnessing the transforming snake, instinctively took out the box hidden in his chest and removed the lotus flower from within. He threw the flower in the direction in which the snake was heading.

They were not trying to fight the snake; they were working with it instead! Could this be Rahu's doing? Was he controlling their minds and using The Defenders to steal Yantra so that he would have the ultimate power?

The snake, now moving at incredible speed, thrust into the air and opened its mouth to grab the lotus flower. As it did so, a wave rose to embrace it. Nereida blew her conch once again, creating a pathway of still water within the turbulent waves. When the snake's body made contact with the water, it instantly transformed into Nessie. As the water flowed across her scaly skin, it morphed her into the sea creature and carried her along the pathway that Nereida had formed. Nessie continued to swim within the current, carrying the sacred gem, still protected in the lotus flower, to Null Island. Eimear and the Siren army were already in the ocean battling the enemies who had entered the Earth through gateways opened in the water. As Nessie made her way with the lotus and Yantra within, the Sirens fought hard to ensure that no enemies would threaten the passage of the sacred gem onto Null Island.

The Energies, who had taken on the appearance of Merpeople, had learnt the Sirens' fighting techniques from previous encounters and mirrored their moves. This made fighting them much more difficult. The aliens, strong and determined, ensured that the Sirens alone would not manage to keep them away from Nessie. To the rescue once again, the monstrous Kraken appeared to fight off the enemy within the water. As it approached, the Kraken created an upsurge of current causing turbulence. The Energies were violently shoved around in the current, giving the Sirens a fighting advantage. While they were at this point away from the shoreline, they were still in shallower water than the ocean depths that the Kraken roamed in. This allowed for a theatrical view of the creature's fighting capabilities. It fought like a bulldozer tearing through rubble as it swung its gigantic appendages.

The Defenders, standing on the shore and looking into the water, came together in an arch parallel to the point of Null

Island. Samara stood at the centre of the arch, Viyan at one end, Ramiel at the other and the rest of the Defenders in between. They each raised their weapons as Ramiel revealed his wings. Samara held her *sword*, Viyan lifted his *trident*, Catori raised her *bow and arrow* and Nereida her *conch*. Liam held up his *spear* while Yana held up his *discus* and Yayali his *mace*. As the Defenders stood on the shore, weapons held up to the sky, their hearts were fully immersed in their purpose and they believed in their cause, in their reason for existence. They knew that they had this one chance to save the World and they owned their power, confident that they were going to win.

Viyan had accepted his destiny and he believed as strongly as the others in his mission. It was this conviction, this individual fervour that connected them at this very moment and that fueled them as a team. The deep, intense, positive belief that they had created an energy within themselves. This energy grew until, through a surge of power, they channelled it from their bodies directly into their weapons. As their weapons charged, Ramiel began to flap his wings, gently at first and then with intense vigour.

All of the weapons that the Defenders held were those very same weapons that Durga carries in her representation. The Goddess was gifted a total of *ten weapons*. These weapons were needed to fight the Energies - the destructive force that Durga protected humans and the Earth from. Each Guardian would carry into battle with them one of these weapons and all ten were needed to vanquish Rahu. The weapons, given to her by the gods, those that she used to protect Man, were the very weapons that the Guardians were using to protect the Earth. The final puzzle piece fit perfectly into place, creating the complete picture.

In the ocean, the Kraken had managed to keep the Energies away from Nessie, allowing an open path for her to swim to Null Island. On land, the Defenders' charged weapons began to glow and they emanated a light to match their suits. The same colours of each of their rooms in Elam. Viyan's trident emitted a *deep, royal-blue* light and Samara's sword a *purple* glow. Catori's bow and the arrows in her quiver generated *green* energy and Nereida's conch had a *turquoise-blue* sparkle. Liam's spear glowed *red* while Yana's discus emanated an *orange* light. Yayali's mace gave off a bright *yellow* shine and Ramiel's wings were outlined with a radiant *burnt-orange* flame.

Yana held the glowing discus in his right hand and rested it on the index finger of his left hand. As it balanced, he began to spin it with his right hand. When he removed his hand, the weapon spun faster and faster upon his finger. As it spun, it started to generate an energy field. Meanwhile, Catori concentrated her efforts on the water. She focused her mind, extracting water from the sea to form a cloud in the air. Once the cloud was formed Yana grabbed the discuss with his right hand and flung it across the ocean. The cloud grew dark and heavy. As Yana released the discus, Ramiel summoned a lightning bolt from the cloud that Catori had formed. He drew the bolt from the air and aimed it at the discus. He fired the bolt and as it hit the weapon, it accelerated it at an incredible speed over the water. Eimear joined Nessie, swimming alongside her. As the discus soared above passed the two, Eimear placed her hand on the monster and transported them at hyper-speed. They now swam parallel to the weapon, all moving in hyper-drive.

The discus made its way over Null Island and to the point above the centre of the Earth. As it reached the centre,

Nessie leapt out of the water and over the discus. Nessie's manoeuvre over the weapon was executed with such precision. As she passed over the discus, she released from her mouth the lotus flower, which landed dead-centre in the discus. The moment the flower moved into the centre of the discus, the two elements jolted stationary, and both fused in the air. The petals of the flower fell away, revealing the sacred gem. Both elements held their place together over Null Island. The discus, now with the gem in the middle, continued to spin over the centre of the Earth creating an energy gateway.

Each of the Defenders was destined over lifetimes to protect the Earth in Durga's image; combined to create her form and unleash her power. As the Defenders stood on the shore in an arch formation, they each held their weapons pointed at an angle toward the sky. The energy from each Guardian, steered through their weapons, blasted into the air. As the force emitted from each weapon aligned with the others, it fused to release a masterful pressure. Ramiel summoned another lightning bolt from the cloud, which he aimed directly at the combined energy coming off from the weapons. The bolt caused the force to ricochet toward the discus and sacred gem. As the burst of energy from the weapons activated the stone, it caused a thrust of power. The force fired straight into the Earth's core – to the centre of the Earth and to Her *heart*. It surged through the Earth's entire core energising and restoring Her. The stream then extended from the Earth's core, back up through the gem and into the sky to the portal. A burst of light encompassed the entire atmosphere surrounding the Earth as if a seal was being placed around the planet. This immediately strengthened the ozone's protective layer surrounding the Earth, healing the hole in the atmosphere and slowly closing the portal. But before the portal closed, the Energies were eliminated. As the Earth's strength was replenished, her positive energy was returned. This force immediately neutralized the Negative Energies and they were rapidly absorbed back into the Universe.

The Defenders watched as the last beams of Energies were pulled into the Universe. They just stood on the shore, not knowing how to react. As they realised their victory, they broke into a cheer, breathing heavy sighs of relief. They turned to hug each other, euphoric from the triumph. Viyan looked at Samara from the opposite end of the group and mouthed to her, "*We did it, we saved the Earth!*"

He was so proud of her, amazed at what his little sister had done. In that moment he did not see her as his little sister but instead the warrior that she was. And he was proud of her fighting spirit and for always believing that they were destined for more. He was grateful to her because he had never felt so accomplished in all of his life. None of his life plans could have resulted in this achievement; to have saved the Earth but also to have discovered himself. He had found a purpose way greater than what he had imagined it was. *A fulfilling end,* he thought to himself.

She smiled at him, still in disbelief. It all happened so fast that the victory had not yet completely registered. As Samara looked at Viyan, his facial expression began to change. The rest of the Defenders cheered and celebrated their victory but Viyan and Samara stood still, locked in time, staring at each other. He knew that something was about to happen, he knew it all along, even before the battle had begun, but he did not want to change any course that would alter their victory.

He smiled and then uttered the words, "*I love you*" to Samara. But before she could ask him what was wrong, he fell to the floor.

It was only when he fell, did Samara realise what had transpired. Behind Viyan stood Rahu. Driven by anger, he stabbed Viyan from behind. Not even the magic of Elam, contained within the suit, could protect him. Rahu pierced Viyan with his dark energy sword and like a disease, it rapidly destroyed all the positive energy within him. Because Viyan was inherently good, in this life and all his ones before, his energetic life force was pure. This would be his weakness. He was instantaneously infected by the strong negative attack from Rahu.

Samara was immovable after witnessing what had happened, and she was the only one that was aware of it. As Viyan fell to the ground Rahu was in full view. Samara shouted for Viyan to protect himself. She ran toward him, but it was too late, the attack was instant. Samara leaned over Viyan trying to process what had just occurred. She looked up at Rahu who stood almost motionless, staring at Viyan; confident, as if with just that one attack, he had won the battle. He wore a long black hooded cloak and beneath that a black armoured suit. They could not see his face because he was masked, but there was a darkness about him, a heavy presence.

Samara did not know what she was up against, but she did not care. She was enraged, a wave of anger so consuming that it took over her. She stood up from beside her brother, all the time maintaining her vision on Rahu. She assumed her warrior pose, akin to an image of Durga about to battle a demon. Fierce, driven, determined. She looked directly at

Rahu and drew her sword, ready to swing at him. But before she could attack, the Defenders pulled her back.

They took control of the situation and worked in an unrehearsed coordinated unison. Yana attacked Rahu. He flashed in and punched him in the face before disappearing. He did this a few times, flashing in and disappearing just as quickly, striking Rahu before he was able to fight back. After receiving a few punches to the face, Rahu realised what Yana was doing. He timed him, and with a powerful swipe of his arm, Rahu hit Yana and sent him flying through the sand. Yayali raced over to ensure that he was alright. Yana's distraction had allowed Catori to create a storm. Ramiel summoned electric bolts from the current and Catori controlled the lightning bolts through guidance from her wind energy. With precision speed, she used the wind to shoot the bolts with full force at Rahu. As she did this, Nereida blew a deafening sound from her conch directly at the dark leader. With the piercing sound targeting only Rahu, he cupped his hands over his ears and fell to his knees. As the bolts hit him, they weakened his power. Liam hurled his spear at Rahu and struck him in his chest, shattering his armour.

Liam, Catori, Ramiel and Nereida stood aside, creating a clear pathway directly toward Rahu. Samara stood a short distance in front of him. Now with a direct view, her rage grew. She ran towards him and as she neared, she somersaulted and then catapulted over, drawing her sword in mid-air. Samara landed directly behind Rahu and before he could react, she ran her katana across his neck, decapitating his head. Rahu's energy was immediately pulled up through the ozone in two separate extractions. First the energy of his head and then that of his body was dispelled out into the Universe.

Samara ran back to Viyan and the Defenders followed, giving her some space. She fell to the ground beside him.

"**V**!!" she bawled. She shook him but there was no breath. The tears poured down her face as she held his head in her lap. "He knew it was coming, I could tell in his eyes. That moment that he was distracted, it was because he learnt of his fate. He knew it was going to happen and he didn't tell me," Samara cried as she held him.

"He knew that we would not have pursued the battle if we were aware of this outcome," Catori agreed as tears slowly fell from her eyes.

"And we needed to fight this battle, we had to do it. He risked his life for this mission," Liam added sorrowfully as he felt his chest tighten.

Samara, Liam, Nereida and Catori knelt beside Viyan, who lay on the sand. Yayali walked Quinn through to stand next to them.

"Abada," he said as he guided Quinn forward.

They tearfully looked up at Yayali, unsure of what he was trying to say.

"What does that mean?" Nereida asked.

"Abada," he said again, gesturing at Quinn.

"*Abada* is the name for the *African unicorn*," Yana explained as he joined them.

"According to folklore, the unicorn has healing powers," Ramiel elaborated with a soft smile. "Its horn neutralises poison - it is like an antidote."

"And this is the one folklore that is actually true," Yana added with a grin.

Quinn walked to the other side of Samara, and she moved back allowing him to lean over Viyan's body. The wound had pierced clean through from his back to his heart. Quinn bowed his head and closed his eyes, his horn positioned directly over the wound. It began to glow, dim at first and then brighter. It was extracting something out of Viyan's body. Quinn absorbed the deadly energy through his horn and the emanating light was blinding. Once he had extracted the lethal poison, he aimed his horn at the sky and released the energy through the portal, mere seconds before it sealed permanently shut.

One of the magical properties of unicorns is that they possess healing and restoration powers. No one knew just how strong the powers were though. Quinn had managed to extract the negative energy, but was it powerful enough to bring Viyan back? They stared, just watching and waiting, no one daring to react. Their hearts raced as the minutes passed. And then they saw it - the wound began to actively heal. Once the negativity was drained from Viyan, his life was slowly restored. But if they had waited any longer, the outcome could have been very different.

Viyan took a deep breath as he gained consciousness. When he opened his eyes, Samara, with tears in hers, grabbed him where he lay and hugged him tight. She gripped him tighter than she knew she possibly could. After a few moments, she pulled back and sternly said to him, "Don't you ever die on me again! I will not allow it! If it weren't for Quinn …" she paused for a few seconds before completing, "Well, I don't want to think about it."

Viyan, feeling completely drained, sat up. He reached out to Quinn who came close to him. They touched heads and Viyan whispered, "Thank you my friend."

The Defenders, feeling both triumphant and relieved, hugged Viyan and welcomed him back. They could now with certainty celebrate their victory. Though not as boisterous as the first time, they hugged and congratulated each other, feeling immense gratitude that they were all victorious and alive.

"So, what now?" Samara asked.

"I think we go back home. I know that all of our families are waiting for us to return," Catori replied.

"And mine is already here," Nereida stated as she looked toward the ocean at her family who had helped win the war. The Defenders walked Nereida toward the sea where Eimear waited with the Siren army to take Nereida back to Atlantis.

"Thank you for all you have done in this battle and throughout the ages. For keeping our waters safe and for guarding our Earth. We are so grateful to you all," Viyan said to the Sirens and Nereida.

"Thank you for protecting us," Samara added.

The Defenders hugged and thanked Nereida. Viyan was the last to say goodbye. She hugged him and let him know through his thoughts that she would miss him dearly. As he pulled away, he looked at her and smiled.

"A part of me will always belong to the sea, *I am the Lord of Water after all,*" Viyan replied to her in thought. He winked at her, and Nereida giggled as she shook her head in agreement.

Viyan handed her the triton. "Please thank your father for trusting me with it."

She nodded and smiled before jumping into the ocean.

They watched the transformational shimmer in the water as Nereida dived in. Her tail flapped out one last time before she swam away.

"Must be how they say goodbye in *Mer*," Samara commented.

The Defenders turned around to walk toward Baby. Samara stayed looking over the water. She moved her gaze toward the direction of Null Island. As she raised her hand to brush the hair away from her face, she spotted the strawberry-coloured birthmark on her palm. She moved her hand to the level of the island in the distance so that the birthmark was in line with the island. She smiled. The heart shape birthmark resembled Yantra, the heart-shaped rose-coloured crystal that restored the balance. She looked back at her palm.

"The pieces were always there," she proclaimed, as she shook her head in amazement. "I guess only in retrospect can you understand why things happen the way they do. *Only once the puzzle is complete can you see the whole picture*," she philosophised out loud.

The energy of the Earth strengthened as the ozone protected Her once again. "The Earth is happy! I can feel Her joy and happiness through Her vibrant, positive energy," Catori expressed as she smiled.

Ramiel closed his eyes, "All of the other Guardians are celebrating our victory," he said as he visualised it.

"How do you know?" Samara asked.

"We can feel Elam calling us back home. The guard is down. I can feel my home once again!" Yana said with utmost joy in his reply to Samara.

"We return now home, we must haste make," Yayali said eagerly.

With the energy levels rising in positive vibrations, the protective guards that were once activated by the older Guardians were now abating. The Defenders were able to be guided to their homes with ease.

"Finally! Back home we go!" Yana exclaimed eagerly.

He held on to the majestic Simha and Yayali and teleported to Elam. In a flash, he was back. "It is glorious!" he yelled happily as he returned. "Right, who is next?"

But before anyone could answer he grabbed Samara and Quinn and vanished. When he returned, without saying a word, he huddled Catori, Viyan and Liam and disappeared. He was so amped and empowered that teleporting for him was once again like breathing.

He came back for the last jump, to return Baby and Ramiel to Elam. Both Ramiel and Yana mounted Baby. "You are going to love it Ramiel … you are going home!" Yana was consumed with such joy, blissfully happy for both himself and Ramiel. After all this time, they could finally return home.

Chapter Eleven

A Victorious Return

Yana transported them to Elam, and when they arrived, they were greeted with a big festival. The Fae were dancing to lively music and food was overflowing everywhere. The Defenders, welcomed with smiles and little fairy hugs and kisses, were being celebrated for their victory. The energy was intense, and the magic flowed freely. Elam was glowing; the trees were greener and the flowers brighter. A shared elation passed throughout the World and connected back to Elam.

As jubilant as the celebrations were, the Defenders left early to regroup and reconcile after the battle. They walked toward the palace, still making sense of the surreal experience. Their conversation had changed, it was not about the battle nor the victory but about how they would return to their lives. *How could they after what they had just experienced?* Life could never be the same, their realities were now altered.

As they approached the castle, they were met by an old man sporting grey hair and a long grey beard.

"Merlin, I presume!" Samara said knowingly as she greeted the man.

The Prince walked in and introduced them, "Defenders, please meet the wise old owl of Elam."

Merlin had mixed a muscle-relaxant bath-elixir which he gifted to the Defenders as a thank you for their victory.

"It is you that we should be thanking," Catori told him as she accepted the vial.

"Yeah, these suits were awesome, their magic protected us in battle," Liam jumped in. "And it was able to morph when I did. Super cool, man!"

"Well … it protected some of us more than others," Viyan said as he rubbed the tear in his suit.

Merlin bent down to trace his fingers over the rip in Viyan's suit.

"Magic can be both dark and light. And sadly, when we allow even a glimmer of fear in, we give way for the dark to manipulate the light."

As he stood upright again, Merlin looked at Viyan and continued. "But as long as there is good in your heart and faith in your soul, no dark can consume you."

That night after they each had a soak, they had the most beautiful of sleeps, knowing that they had accomplished the impossible and fulfilled their purpose. The next morning as the light hit their rooms, they awoke feeling brand new, fully recovered and with not a scratch on them. The elixir had repaired them as they slept. Except for Viyan, whose death scar remained. A war tattoo and a reminder of the sacrifice of a Guardian.

They made their way down for breakfast where a feast awaited. Their bodies must have used up all of their remaining energy to heal because they were famished. The taste of the food was indescribable. If at all possible, it was even more spectacular than the first time. They recounted the battle for the Prince. It sounded as if they were describing the plot to an action movie and the Prince was utterly enticed. They sat for hours at the table before the conversation eventually died down. They knew that it was time to return to their homes and to their families. It was bittersweet to leave the table because this was most likely the last time that they would see each other.

Prince Caden walked them out of the castle. As they approached the point of exit from Elam, the tension in the air was amplified by their silence. Samara held Quinn and Simha as they walked, aware that she would have to leave them behind.

"How will we be able to come back to visit? How can I come to see them?" she asked Prince Caden.

"You will know," he assured her.

"Now that the balance is restored, we do not need to be so heavily protected. We will still need to remain hidden from the rest of the world for our safety, but we will not be hidden from you. Once you have settled back into your life, if you ever want to visit, your instincts will guide you."

"A little vague as always but ok, I trust you," she said, accepting the Prince's answer.

As they reached the tree to leave, the crowd had gathered to bid them farewell. Samara held on tightly to Quinn and they touched heads and shared a connected moment. She did the same with Simha. She bid farewell to Prince Caden, Ramiel, Yana and the people of Elam, shedding tears as she turned around to walk out. Catori, Viyan and Liam also said their goodbyes, hugging the Prince and their fellow Guardians who would remain in Elam.

Viyan, Samara, Liam and Catori left Elam together and Yayali walked them out through the tree, almost not wanting for them to leave. But he stopped just before they took their steps outside of Elam. They hugged the gentle giant before entering back into the forest.

Viyan turned to him, "Thank you, my friend," he said before walking out to join Catori, Liam and Samara. But when he turned around once again, the pathway in the tree to Elam had closed. As they stared at the tree, which now looked the same as every other tree in the forest, Samara said, "I know that it's a tad bit late to ask but how will we ever find the portal to Elam again?"

Catori responded, "Do not worry, if you ever need them, they will find you."

They were now back on American soil. But this also meant that they all had to go their separate ways. Walking a few steps together in silence, they could get the feel of the land. Catori stopped to place her hands on one of the trees. She closed her eyes to feel the energy of the forest so as to gain her bearings. "We are about a few miles away from my reservation, in this direction," she said as she pointed to her right.

"I guess that means that I am in the opposite direction," Liam said with a heavy voice. "Makes sense for me to head off on my own then."

The others did not reply, it was rather difficult for them all to be going separate ways.

Viyan walked up to Liam. "Thank you, brother. For welcoming us, for being so genuine and for making this whole crazy experience a bit lighter than it would have been."

Samara grabbed Liam in a tight embrace. "I am going to miss you so much. I will look you up on social media."

Catori also hugged him goodbye. "I must say, you are quite likeable for a Lycan."

Liam smiled at her as they came out of the hug. "And thank you for admitting that I am better than you are Cat," he replied. And before Catori could retort, he transformed into a wolf and sprinted back home.

The remaining three began to make their way back to the reservation. As they walked, Catori spotted a few birds flying through the trees. She called to one of them to come down and whispered to it as it rested on her hand. The bird flew off and they continued walking, following Catori's lead, as if talking to wild birds was now the norm. They discussed the battle and what the triumph meant for the World, but they also thought about what it meant for them.

"I wonder if our lives will change much now?" Viyan questioned.

"Well, it won't change, not in terms of fame or anything, no one even knows what we have done," Samara responded.

"I won't even be able to tell my friends!" Viyan lamented.

"To be honest, no one cares," Catori remarked. "The World will for the most go on as it has, not many will even notice the change."

"Wow, all of that and it won't even impact anyone," Samara sighed.

"But it will make an impact! My grandfather will explain it to us." Catori replied as if she knew that someone was there to get them. They heard movement among the trees and then galloping. Their horses had come to transport them back.

Another celebration awaited them at Catori's village. The tribe welcomed them with a triumphant greeting in song and food. They accepted the blessings and tributes from the tribesmen. A group of little girls walked up shyly to Samara to offer her a headpiece. Samara was touched and bent her head for one of the girls to put it on. This was a significant gesture as the tribe had welcomed Samara and Viyan into their clan. The chief presented the same to Viyan.

"Thank you," Viyan said, as he looked at the Chief.

Viyan didn't have to say anything more, the Chief knew what he wanted to convey and he acknowledged it with a smile and a nod of his head.

After spending a while with the tribesmen, the Chief motioned for them to follow him. "The sun is beginning to set and soon it will be dark. You must be excited to go home," he expressed. As they walked toward his tent, they witnessed a dark shadow eclipsing the moon. It was clearly visible in the limpid skies of Kaya. They stopped to watch the shadow move across the moon.

"*Ketu!*" the Chief uttered.

In his tent, the Chief thanked them for their courage and victorious win in defeating Rahu.

"Is he vanquished? Did we manage to destroy him?" Samara asked.

"The balance has been restored but because he is immortal, Rahu cannot be permanently destroyed. *Ketu* eclipsing the moon tells us that he is still close. They both represent *the negative* and remember, the positive cannot exist without it."

"*There are more Rahus*!?" Samara exclaimed, confused by the sudden introduction of this Ketu character.

"It is a little complicated, but they are essentially two elements of one whole," the Chief explained.

"Yes! That clarifies it," she replied sarcastically.

"You may not have eliminated Rahu, but you have successfully stopped him, and that was your mission all along. It is up to humans to now protect the Earth and to change the trajectory of their destructive ways. That is important!" He looked at the three. "Man will not know what has happened. Only if the results had gone the other way would the world have known of the disaster because it would have directly affected them. But now there is no visible outcome so the humans will never know what you have done."

"I don't understand though," Samara said shaking her head. "What was the point of all of this? How will we humans ever change our ways if we do not know what fate could have possibly fallen on the Earth? The world will just keep on... on the same path, and humans will just become more destructive," she sighed irritably, feeling hopeless.

The Chief smiled and replied to her, "Humans are good at their inner-most, at their core, it is in their being. When born into an environment that is negative, this is what we are exposed to, and it is what we learn. We experience the world in this way, and we think that this is how we should be. It is all we know, but it is not who we are. It takes only a few to change that negativity. Just like it can take one bad apple to turn the whole basket - like what eventually happened to the World - it also takes one flame to bring light to the dark."

The Chief took Samara's hand. "Don't worry child, the World is changing. There are so many candles being lit, so many awakening to their purpose and their truth. Man is lighting a new way. Humans may not know what happened, but they sure will feel it, and they will see the impact around them. There is so much positivity radiating from the Earth, it is difficult not to feel it."

They were comforted by the Chief's words and felt a sense of pride in what they had accomplished.

"So? Now that our purpose is achieved, do we just go back to our normal lives?" Samara asked. She felt unsure of herself now. How could she just return to her boring life of limbo? Back to all of that uncertainty, not knowing where she fit in or what to do - back to feeling rejected and incomplete.

"No!" The Chief smiled. "You need to remember this; even though you have prevented a fatal disaster by stopping Rahu from consuming and destroying our Earth, you have not eliminated all the negativity. With every *ying* there needs to be a balanced *yang,* and because negativity is necessary, it will always exist. And so, we as the Guardians will always need to ensure that this balance is maintained and that neither energy becomes too dominant to the extent of destruction. Perhaps you will be called upon in this lifetime to restore this balance or perhaps the next. The one thing that I can be sure of though, is that we are all not done learning our lessons. And because of this, the *scales* of good and evil, negative and positive, *will always dance.*"

Viyan, Samara and Catori felt a sense of relief that they would possibly be seeing their newfound family again. But for now, they had a lot of personal reflection and understanding to do. Samara paused for a moment and thought. She was definitely not the same person who left her home, so the life that she was afraid to return to did not exist anymore. She had a new lease on life, and she now knew that she was never a *nobody*, she was just somebody who needed to find herself. And while she did not know it then, she was *always more than enough*. Through this journey she discovered that she was never going to find her purpose in others. And at the end of it, she had finally found it in herself.

Viyan and Samara were ready to return home to their parents. The Chief called on some of his tribespeople who had assimilated into the modern world to drive the siblings back home. Samara hugged Catori and thanked her for showing her the way and for helping her find her purpose. Catori gifted Samara with a dreamcatcher, "So that you always have good dreams that guide your way and help you find your path."

"Thank you so much!" Samara was completely moved by the gesture and by Catori's intuition.

"And I am always here if you need to talk, just reach out to me."

Samara was certain that Catori didn't mean on a cellphone, but she would figure it out.

Catori walked up to Viyan, and like the first time he saw her, her eyes pierced into his soul. And just like the first time, his heart skipped a beat. In his newfound bravery, he knew that a hug goodbye would not suffice. He moved forward to kiss her, and it was the most beautiful feeling. The boy who had his life mapped out was struck off course. In that kiss, he instantly knew that his life had a new purpose. Catori was ready to learn more about Viyan's world and now that she had met the other Guardians, she was not as cynical as before. She promised that she was going to visit them. Now that her mission was done, she could return to the modern world.

Ahh, maybe she did mean with a cellphone, Samara thought to herself.

Viyan and Samara jumped into the Jeep of the tribespeople there to drive them back. A little exhausted, they slept the entire way home and were woken as they reached their house. Nervous to see their parents and not knowing what to say, they paused at the door. Samara looked at Viyan and then rang the doorbell. Her mum answered. Completely stunned, it took a few seconds for their presence to register. She screamed for their dad before bursting into tears. She grabbed both of her children and hugged them tightly before their dad bolted down the stairs to join in.

As they entered the house their mum immediately walked into the kitchen to prepare a warm meal. Viyan and Samara joined her, no one saying a word but keeping each other company. It was too awkward for anyone to say anything, no one even knew where to begin. Samara eventually broke the silence by saying that she was going to her room for a shower.

"Me too!" Viyan followed.

"Don't be too long, the food will be ready in a few minutes."

It was so good to be back in their own house and to have a shower again. They both felt like wilderness explorers who hadn't bathed in a month. Despite all the various dwellings over the past few days, nothing could compare to the comfort of home.

Once refreshed, they headed back down to the kitchen to join their parents. Completely in awe, their mum stared at them and excitedly shrieked, "Tell me everything!"

And they did ... every last detail.

Chapter Twelve

The End Just Means
A New Beginning

Life resumed, and it was back to the normal routine. Viyan and Samara returned to work, but they knew that they would not stay there for very long. Samara decided to apply to teach in Africa for a year, once her schooling was complete. She felt repurposed and no longer stuck. Samara had a new appreciation for her existence and a desire to learn as much as she could in her new zest for life. She was no longer trying to belong but instead yearning to explore and experience the world; the World that she helped save.

Viyan was always driven to excel in his education and his career. But having learnt about his past and more about who he used to be, it gave him a fresh appreciation for life and how he wanted to live it. He wanted less structure, he wanted to escape and explore the world with Catori, to experience it from her perspective. While they had these plans for the near future, they had to settle back into their normal lives in the meantime. Viyan resumed the weekly routine with his friends. Although he had to lie to them about where he had disappeared to, he was so tempted to share the truth with them. Perhaps in time he would.

A month after their return home, they fell back into ordinary, almost forgetting how their lives had been turned upside down. But life never derails without teaching you a few lessons. Samara continued to be friends with Megan, but she knew how to control her emotions now. She was no longer seeking anyone's approval or their company and this allowed her to experience relationships and people so much better than before. She had a newfound confidence and life had become full of opportunities; an adventure to experience. And every time that she would forget, she would take one look at her katana - *a reminder of her bravery and strength.*

Several months later, when things were stable again, Samara began to experience a persistent uneasiness. One night she woke in a panic, completely out of breath from a dream she had had. She sat up in her bed, gazing at the wall, trying to process what she had dreamt.

Durga had returned; but this time she was joined by the *goddess Kali.* Though beautiful, with her long flowing locks and rich, dark skin, the Goddess exuded a heavy energy about Her, an energy which Samara interpreted as fear. And she had everything to fear, for Kali was known as the Dark Mother, the *Goddess of Death and Time.*

Just as Samara calmed herself down, Viyan burst through her room door. Frozen in place he stared directly at her.

"OH NO! Not again!" she exclaimed.

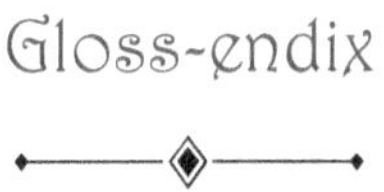

Glossary meets Index

This section is mainly a glossary to explain a few of the words used, but it is also an Index to clarify certain media references and certain bits of information from the story. *It's basically an Appendix.* But there are no maps, because, although I did contemplate adding one, I'm really bad at drawing.

These explanations are mostly my interpretation of information that I have learnt or researched. And if any points do interest you, Google! (she advised with a nod of her head).

Abada

Abada is thought of as the African *unicorn*, but it has two horns instead of one. Legend says that the horns of the Abada can act as an antidote to poison and disease.

Atlanteans

The name of the people from the fictional Atlantis.

Atlantis

A mythical city theorised by the philosopher Plato to have existed some 11600 years ago. Plato described Atlantis as a rich, advanced society that sunk to the bottom of the sea.

Barbie

The fashion doll that become an icon and influenced global culture. The Barbie adverts of the 90s personified Barbie as if she really had a life of her own and this is what Samara imagines.

Big Foot

Aka Sasquatch, aka Yeti, is a big, hairy, ape like creature rumoured to live in the wild. A few sightings have been reported in North America with versions of the creature believed to exist in Asia and Australia. For now, it remains a legend as no proof of its existence has been verified.

Bruce All Mighty

A 2003 film staring Jim Carrey as Bruce. After complaining to Morgan Freeman, who plays God, Bruce gets to be Him for a week. The movie takes a comedic look at what it would be like to be God.

Chupacabra

One of the younger legends, this myth began in the mid-nineties. Translated, the word means *goat-sucker* and describes a creature that would kill animals through the consumption of their blood via small puncture wounds.

Defenders

This is the name that the young Guardians choose for themselves to differentiate them from all the other Guardians of Earth.

Durga

Durga is a Hindu goddess who represents strength, protection and motherhood. Some consider Durga the *supreme goddess* from which other goddesses (or forms of Her) manifested. This is why She is considered the Mother Goddess. Durga also represents war through the destruction of evil, and the liberation of the oppressed. A title that was given to Her post the slaying of the demon *Mahishasura*.

Durga's Weapons

For Her battle with Mahishasura, Durga was gifted ten weapons by the gods. Each weapon has symbolic meaning:

- *Bow and Arrow* – They represent energy and symbolise power and control.

- *Conch Shell* – This represents connection. The shell symbolises the primordial sound of Om, which reminds one of God. The sound has the power to destroy negative energies.

- *Club /Mace* – Symbolises the destroying of evil and the absence of fear.

- *Discus* – Represents creation. Always spinning, it is a reminder of change and to keep revolving.

- *Lotus* – The lotus represents the triumph of good over evil as the flower remains pure despite growing in mud. The lotus is also symbolic of wisdom and knowledge.

- *Spear* – Represents the ability to overcome obstacles.

- *Thunderbolt* – This represents firmness in character and belief in one's convictions.

- *Sword* – The sword represents knowledge and truth and the wisdom to know right from wrong. A double-edged sword could also represent the duality of positive and negative.

- *Trident* – The three points of the trident represent past, present and future. The weapon symbolizes control of time.

Drakensburg

A mountain range in South Africa that forms part of the Great Escarpment. Translated to English, the name means *Dragon Mountains*.

Elam

A fictional land that is home to the Fae. Elam means Forever/ Eternal.

 *There is no relation to the fallen Iranian Empire.

Energies

The name given to describe the aliens that the Guardians must battle to save Earth.

Fae

The collective name for the people of Elam. They include fairies, pixies and elves, among others.

Guardians of Earth

These are the ancient groups and individuals who were selected to protect the Earth. Each have different roles to ensure the safety and survival of the Earth.

Jumanji: The Next Level

The third instalment to the cult classic. Samara refers to a specific scene where the characters switch avatars and learn new traits in the process.

Kali

The Hindu goddess that represents death and time. Kali is known as the *Dark Mother*. While She may appear ferocious, Kali is protective and Her portrayed destructive nature is such to signify her elimnation of evil.

Khal

From the series Game of Thrones, Khal comes from the fictional language of the Dothraki and means King or Leader.

Khaleesi

Also derived from Game of Thrones, Khaleesi means Queen but is also the title of the *Mother of Dragons*.

Kraken

The gigantic mythical monster that is believed to live in the deepest darkest waters. The legend originates from Norwegian writings. It is likened to an octopus and is said to have destroyed ships and killed many a sailor.

Lightening Bird

The Lightening Bird, a South African legend, is similar to the North American legend *Thunderbird*. It is a supernatural being associated with power and strength and the creature is said to be able to summon lightening with a flap of its wings.

Listen

A 2007 song by Beyonce featured in the movie Dreamgirls.

Loch Ness Monster

A creature from Scottish folklore believed to have lived in Loch Ness. Theories have suggested that the creature could be a dinosaur, but no conclusive proof of the monster's existence has been found.

Lycan

A human who has the ability to transform into a wolf, usually at the sight of a full moon. The Greek legend of Lycaon could be where the myth began. While there have been claims of sightings, this legend exists mainly within pop culture.

Mary Poppins Nursery

This references the scene from the classic movie Mary Poppins in which the nanny uses magic to help the children 'tidy up' their room.

Mer-people / Merfolk

A worldwide known myth that focuses on water creatures that are half-human, half-fish, with the upper body of a woman or man and the tail of a fish. Different cultures may have their own versions of the exact description but Merfolk remain a myth, although many people have tried to prove their existence.

Mina Moo

A South African children's educational programme that centred around a dairy-cow puppet called Mina Moo.

NAfAEAuAsSA

The fictional native language of the Shamanic People.
This language is an acronym for the names of Earth's continents; North America, Africa, Antarctica, Europe, Australia, Asia, South America.

Null Island

While a fictional island, Null Island's location actually marks the very centre of the Earth. It is the exact point where the prime meridian and the equator intersect. Zero degrees latitude and zero degrees longitude with the co-ordinates 0°N 0°E.

Portals

These are the openings to the other worlds. Portals allow for the Negative Energies from outside of Earth to gain access to, and enter onto, the planet.

Rahu

One of the nine celestial bodies, Rahu is considered a shadow planet. It is thus associated with negativity. Rahu is usually paired with another shadow planet called *Ketu*. According to legend, were both formed when the demon Svarbhanu was beheaded.

Rooibos Tea

An all-natural South African tea.

Sari

Traditional dress worn by many women from South Asian countries.

Shamanic People

The fictional group of people who form part of the Guardians. They have the ancient knowledge on natural healing and natural magic.

Simha

Simha is the name of Durga's lion. It is short for *Mahasimha*. Simha is also the Sanskrit name for the Zodiac sign Leo.

Siren

The word Siren stems from Greek mythology and refers to alluring sea creatures with captivating voices. Sirens were initially thought to be half-woman, half-bird, but the legend evolved to them being half-fish instead, like a mermaid.

The Little Mermaid

A Danish fairytale written in 1837 by Hans Christen Anderson. It was adapted into the classic Disney animated movie which Samara references a scene from.

The Threat

The Threat refers to the destruction that will befall Earth. It marks the time when Rahu will enter the planet's atmosphere and it ultimately leads to the *great battle* that the Guardians are destined to fight.

The Twilight Zone

An American series which originally aired in 1959. Each episode would feature characters experiencing strange occurrences described as entering *The Twilight Zone.*

Tokoloshe

A South African legend that describes a small in stature, prank playing individual. Like most legends, the evolution of the myth suggests that the creature is evil and malicious.

Tree of Secrets

The entrance into Elam. The Tree of Secrets is a giant oak tree on the outside but inside it provides the passageway that one must walk through to reach Elam.

Unicorn

A legendary horse like creature with a horn on its head. Usually portrayed in children's stories, unicorns have been adapted into mainstream media. Some believe that its horn has magical properties.

The Sea Voyage

I will be honest, every time that I edited chapter 6 (which was many, many times), I would have to go back to the map to ensure that I had charted this journey correctly. So, to explain it for the last time (this is more for my reference than yours really) here it is:

- The Sirens meet the Guardians on the coast of North Carolina.

- They swim to the Atlantic Ocean and are transported to Atlantis.

- Atlantis is in the Mediterranean Sea.

- After visiting Atlantis and picking up Nereida and the triton, they continue on their journey.

- From Atlantis they move through the Strait of Gibraltar, back into the Atlantic Ocean.

- Then, they travel into the Celtic Sea and finally end their sea voyage in the Irish Sea.

*When I read this voyage sequence, I imagine an ancient, animated treasure map that plots the journey with dotted lines and arrows, and a little ship that stops to pick up Nereida and the triton. Try it, it makes it less complicated.